The Crypt of Lost Souls

Molly R. Anderson

This book is a work of fiction.
The author in no way represents the companies, corporations, or brands mentioned in this book. The likeness of historical/famous figures have been used fictitiously; the author does not speak for or represent these people. All opinions and specific events in this book are the author's or fictional.

Cover by Molly Anderson

Self-Published

First Edition: September 2025
ISBN: 9798999870704 (paperback)
ISBN: 979-8-9998707-1-1 (hardback)
ISBN: 979-8-9998707-2-8 (ebook)

Printed in the USA

*To my husband, who has been my greatest support.
I love you.*

Prologue

I'm not really sure when it started when I look back. Now I was sitting alone in my apartment whispering to a flashlight. How the hell did I end up here? What the hell was I trying to do? Who was I even trying to invite in?

Sitting alone in my apartment, in my office, at night, with nothing but a flashlight sitting on my desk. I don't know why I sometimes chose to do these things when I did. It was never really 'prime' timing. It was always just, I have a few free minutes and I'm alone, so let's just test it out.

I still couldn't bring myself to do it around anyone but my sister. Try to speak to anyone. To be fair, I think the idea seemed fun to some people but probably only when you were watching it on a screen and not actually living it. I, for some strange reason, wanted the experience. Thankfully, my sister was the one other person who also did.

But, right now, she wasn't with me. I was on my own, back in my office, with the flashlight. Whenever I tested this out I was expecting it not to work, waiting for it not to work, hoping it wouldn't. I always started with the same first question. "Is anyone there that would like to talk?" Then wait.

I had done this a few times now, it was always pretty easy going, until now. Whatever came through this time was not happy. Or maybe it was happy to finally make a connection, but it definitely shouldn't be. I didn't know what the hell this thing was.

Chapter 1

It started with a flicker, my eyes widening in disbelief. It's working? How could it already be working?

Standing alone in my dining room, which lined up directly in front of the kitchen—separated only by a large counter space and two barstools—I was barely able to move, barely able to breathe.

I had grabbed the flashlight in the few minutes after Wes left. He had gone out with a friend so I didn't have a lot of time. I had the chance alone and I just had to give it a try. In no world did I think it would actually work!

I was standing several feet away from where the light now sat on the counter, no one else was home, nothing was plugged in near me, nothing was on or running in the kitchen. There was nothing to explain what was happening.

I asked another question. On again, then off.

I grabbed the light and moved into the living room. Maybe the coffee table would be different. It was an ottoman so there was fabric—cushion. Hard enough to balance a light and far enough from everything that I could be sure. I set the light down and waited. Nothing. Until I asked the question again, "Is someone there?" On. There wasn't even hesitation.

This all began within minutes of trying. Wes had walked out the door maybe ten minutes ago!

I had seen other people try this. Obviously, I needed to learn how to do it properly and that took a little bit of research. But everything I'd seen started off much longer. Sometimes it even needed some sort of offering or bribe. I had nothing but my presence.

Me, myself, and I. Alone, at night, sitting on the floor of my now dimly lit living room—staring at my ottoman in shock. What do I do now?

I grabbed my phone and texted my sister. Turning my phone to record, the light was still on. "Ok, you can turn the light off now please." Snap. Off.

"What the fuck?" I texted her. "Is my place haunted? Did I bring something home?"

I was terrified to say the least. But why was I also strangely calm? I didn't even know what I was sitting in the presence of. Was it good? Was it evil? Either way something was there.

It wasn't touching me, I didn't feel it watching me, it was just there. Only telling me through the switch of the light.

Was it in another room? Was it in the same room and just focused on the light? Could it control the light from a distance?

I was thinking too much. Still frozen, I proceeded, "Do you want to speak with me?" Light on, waited a moment and back off. Whatever was there was waiting for the next question.

It was fast enough that I could barely even process before continuing, "Have you been with me for a while?" Light back on. Another yes.

"Do you live here?" No response. But I couldn't quite tell if it was a no or if it didn't want to answer.

I hated that I could only ask yes or no questions with my limited resources. The limited function of a damn flashlight.

"Are you friendly?" I felt like I already knew the answer. The light remained off.

"Do you have bad intentions?" Instantly on. Flat out yes.

"Are you trying to scare me?" Another yes.

"Are you human?" Remained off, "Then you can leave. Negative energy is not welcome here." The light remained off.

"Are you still here?" On. "Leave. This conversation is over."

I snatched the light and turned it off completely, severing any and all remaining contact. I still had so many questions, but there was no way I was getting answers, not tonight at least. I didn't want to even try.

I simply sat, holding the light, trying to digest and process everything that had just happened. What I had been the only witness to.

The air felt heavy. When using the light I hadn't felt any actual presence looking at me, watching me, trying to touch me, or reach me. Now, all I felt was watchful eyes, waiting for my next move. What the hell could I have just done? What could I have possibly just allowed in? Even without a direct invitation, and telling it to leave, I didn't know what it was.

I needed answers, I just wasn't even sure of all the answers I needed.

"Is it still going off?" My phone started buzzing at my sister's text. Luckily I had been able to record a chunk of the interaction. Though I may have left out a few questions. So I sent her the video.

She didn't respond right away. I knew, even without being here, even she didn't know how to react.

"Maybe you should stop for tonight." She responded. "Any idea who it was?"

"No clue…I don't even know that it was a 'who'. It might not have been human."

"What would it be if not human?"

"I stopped for tonight. I have no idea what it would be but let's talk about it later."

"You need to get some crystals!"

Why did I want to try again though? I still felt a presence. Whatever I had connected with was still with me, but I was not about to reopen that door. Not without some preparation. I needed to figure out how to make sure it disconnected and if I couldn't do that, figure out how to get rid of it completely.

Still holding the flashlight, I got myself up and put it away, grabbing my book instead. I wanted to get lost in something else. I couldn't focus on a feeling or a sense I just needed to disappear until Wes got home.

I didn't mention anything to Wes. I was still processing and although we had seen clips and videos together of other people sharing experiences, I knew he would still be skeptical. I wasn't prepared to be defensive. I didn't want to be defensive. You just had to be there. I already felt silly but that wasn't going to feel better coming from someone else.

This was the first time trying anything on my own.

Or, if he also believed it, would he be upset that I tried it at home? That was probably a bad idea—I'll admit that. But I didn't even know if I actually needed to fix anything yet. So no need to worry him yet. Those were really the only two reactions I could see happening.

So I stayed quiet about it and tried to enjoy the relief of no longer being alone.

Chapter 2

Thankfully Wes had work the next morning. I had still spoken no word of what had happened the night before. I wasn't ready to relive any of it. I especially wasn't ready to give any explanation of why I was trying to do what I did. There was no real explanation other than curiosity and to be fair, I didn't think it would work. Not in my own house.

I was just relieved to not have any nightmares the night before. As long as I can remember I've always had extremely vivid dreams, good or bad. Most of the time, I at least knew I was dreaming, but that didn't keep it from still feeling any less real. It didn't mean I could stop anything from happening. Of course, stress was usually the trigger and I never knew what my brain would cook up at night, but luckily nothing came. I slept through the night. Probably the peace of not going to sleep alone brought some comfort to relieve that.

I always woke up before Wes. I worked from home so I needed to have a short time to myself in the morning to wake up and have my coffee before helping him get ready to leave.

And though my sister lived across the country, 3 hours ahead, she knew I'd be awake early. As crazy as it may sound to some, I'm always awake by 5 AM to have my 'me' time. Wes has to be out the door by 6:15.

"So, any idea what to think about last night?" My phone buzzed and lit up to show Maia's text.

"Honestly, I'm still processing... Either nothing, a fluke that I can't explain yet, or...I'm screwed." I responded and headed to the kitchen.

Most people normally have their morning coffee sitting at the dining table or in the living room, but my office had become my space. When Wes wasn't home I was barely even in the living room. I had my computer, my notebooks, my books, my phone stand, all in my office. So however I wanted to spend that wake up me time was already right there.

I loved my office. I had never had a dedicated office room before this apartment. The places I lived in before weren't bad, they had enough space. But the desk space was always right there in the rest of the it, no separation. Now it wasn't only keeping my work separate but it was also my own little separate area from the rest of the apartment. Wes loved to laugh and call it my lair like I'm some witch! But always joking.

"Gonna go hide in your lair?" He'd make a face at me.

It's a longer story of how we ended up in this apartment but it was the biggest apartment I'd ever had.

My last place wasn't tiny, but in this one, it was technically a two-bedroom, so we were able to turn the second room into my office. Something I specifically wanted.

I had finished my coffee and was wrapping up Wes' lunch, my small help while he finished getting ready to leave. Walking over to bring it to the door while he was getting on his shoes.

I was clearly distracted but luckily he is always still waking up and too tired to really notice that on his way out the door.

He's one of those people that doesn't really take any time in the morning to wake up. He'd rather sleep as much as possible, get up, get ready and head out the door.

"Love you, hope you have a good day." He gave me a kiss and headed out.

Almost a little guilty I was right back to my phone as soon as the door shut, "Should I try again?"

"Just to see if it's still lingering or maybe see if it left altogether?" I clarified in a second message.

"...I don't know." One message. Great.

"Do you think if it's still there you'll be able to find out what it is?" She sent another.

"I think...I think I'll either find out what it is or just that it's bad and will lie about everything."

I knew I officially sounded crazy. But from everything I read that's all I could go off of. Why would I feel like I knew what I was doing just because I'd seen other people who go ghost hunting?

I didn't know if I felt like that anymore or if I just felt compelled to know more. But I felt calm last night, I was in shock and couldn't believe what was happening, but I was calm, why?

I'd always been interested in this stuff, in the paranormal. I think I got the initial interest from my mom. Which, funny enough, I think even she realized she was more into the fun of it, but the idea of experiencing anything herself, that massively freaked her out.

She always had ghost stories and loved spooky things, but the recent interests my sister and I were having, she was more wishing us luck and fun from afar.

But, that long time interest and fascination still didn't explain the calm. The strange calm understanding that something was there, something was present. It didn't tell me what it was, who it was, how it got there, or how long it had been here. But it wasn't going to hurt me. For some reason, I knew that much. I just knew I couldn't allow it to touch me. That would be the wrong move.

But still, maybe I should play this smarter. I didn't know what had just happened, I didn't even know if it wasn't just some unexplainable fluke. Because literally, how do you explain that? The light is turning on and off, not only by itself, but only in time with me asking yes or no questions? And the answer wasn't even yes every time. I could maybe argue a fluke if it was a constant yes because of timing, but it wasn't. Some was even flickers and some on switches were snapped! But now I was just working myself up again at the thought.

"I definitely need to do it while I'm alone. But I just need to think about this more first. I should probably also do a little research." I texted my sister finally. I'd gone back into the kitchen and hadn't left since Wes had left for work. Just standing there, leaning against the counter, contemplating.

"I definitely need to do it while I'm alone. I just need to think first." I followed up my last text. I wasn't ready to just run back to my office, grab the light out of the drawer, and jump back in.

Neither one of us expected these things to work for us. This was like a new random hobby, a fun interest. The first time I saw anyone sharing proof online about an actual haunted location is what really started piquing my interest. I've seen things randomly pop up here and there but usually it's easily explained or clearly staged, like random activity or a door slowly closing or slamming shut. This time was different. This time they were showing history, which also grabbed my attention. Talking about actual experiences from other people who may or may not know about the history of the location. In some cases it was even like solving some mystery that was left open-ended or told inaccurately. It was all so intriguing.

But, that was at least a year ago now. Something I shared with Maia and we both went down the rabbit hole. We both wanted to know if there really could be more out there, if it could be possible to connect. It was a fun, spooky idea.

We decided we wanted to see for ourselves and actually started looking into which locations we wanted to visit. Though, obviously, we couldn't jump on a plane or get in the car and start going everywhere, we wanted to start getting the gadgets. Prepare for our first ghost hunting trip when we were ready. However, the downside of that, you might want to try out some of the gadgets before you get to a location. The locations you expect them to work at, where you hope they work. Leaving you in your kitchen, with a single flashlight, that just turned itself on and then back off.

"That might be the smartest move. Just wait a bit, see if you're still comfortable." I knew my sister was just as curious as me, but trying that light again was just too much.

What a hell of a night and morning already.

Wes had left so I grabbed my own breakfast and headed back down the hall, for the office again. The light had gone back into the drawer. Somehow that made it feel more contained.

I just needed to try and concentrate on work. At least I didn't feel anything anymore. Maybe it was just something silly, just getting to my nerves. I was anxious and hyperaware but still felt nothing now.

So I sat at my desk and woke up my computer, my attempt to get on with the actual day ahead. My dog sleeping peacefully in her bed just behind me, another good sign. So I carried on, forgetting about the little spirit wand just sitting in wait behind me.

At least they couldn't actually move things right?

The next several hours were a strain if I'm honest. My brain was being pulled in multiple directions. An hour into work I'd find myself having a distant thought, leading to a google search, leading to a rabbit hole. Never really coming up on anything because I didn't really know what I was looking for.

This needed to wait for the weekend. Wes' schedule had recently changed so now we had more time in the afternoons together. This already happened sometimes where there were other things I needed to get done during the day so work priorities would get pushed back a bit. Then I'd end up working after he got home. He never said anything or that he cared, would even sometimes say he didn't. But I did know that it bothered him.

But I could ask for a little help.

"Hey, I can't keep trying to look into anything for now. I don't know if I can at all today." I texted Maia, I needed the help, I needed the mental break if I could even imagine the possibility of trying again this weekend. "Can you take a look and see what you can find?"

"On it. I have meetings this afternoon but I can take a look after work." She responded within minutes.

Some sense of relief.

The research itself even felt a little like WebMD. The more I looked the more I felt like I'd find something eventually to tell me, your place is haunted, you're haunted, you have something attached, and you'll most likely end up possessed. Good luck! There's nothing to show anything has fully fixed these problems. No cure.

So I could use a little help taking my mind off it to say the least.

For now, I could try getting through the day. Which, with Maia's assistance, became a little easier.

Wes goes into work every day, so it was just me at home with our dog Bambi. I worked from home, running a business I started almost 3 years ago. A nerve-wracking move when I first made the leap, also depending on who you asked, but I had never looked back.

On most days, working from home was the better option for me. On a normal day, it was the more productive and creative option. I actually started my business coming out of the pandemic. When Covid first happened, I worked for another company, but we all got sent home to start working remotely. When we started coming out, they wanted us to come back to the office. My particular job didn't need an office space and it was too distracting for me. So here I am, I decided I could be my own boss and build something for myself from home.

However, today was not one of those normal productive creative days. Today I found myself simply staring at my to do list rather than actually completing the tasks.

I wasn't overwhelmed with fear. I wasn't still in shock. I couldn't stop thinking about last night, that was for sure. But in these moments, sitting at my desk, trying to complete work for my clients, make my lunch, thinking about getting dinner ready later...it all just felt so mundane. But wasn't that the point? Those were all normal things people did. It was supposed to keep my mind busy, keep me distracted when I thought I was going to have an anxiety attack. Now I was just annoyed.

I was distracting myself because I let fear get the best of me. Did I need to get these other, now mundane feeling, tasks done? Yes. But did I also need to let them keep me from understanding what had just happened? No. What was it I discovered?

There was no more fear, now I was only determined.

Unfortunately, I knew some research was not going to be able to start until later or tomorrow. Wes would be home soon and it had only been a day. I still didn't have a full grasp on anything so I wasn't ready to explain any of this or my plans yet.

All I could really do for now was look up the safest precautions to take if I was going to try that flashlight again. I had it, I was going to use it, but you know, safety first.

I quickly looked into as much as I could on warding bad energy, protections, crystals, herbs, I was no expert but after last night I'd take any advice I could get. If I use everything at least one thing should be helpful. I took my notes and that's about what I had time for before Wes got home.

"Hey! Any ideas for dinner?"

"Hey, I'm thinking pizza." I said, already pulling out my phone to greet him at the door. Cooking was the last thing on my mind.

"Sounds great." He said and gave me a kiss, pulling his shoes off at the door.

Chapter 3

Life this week felt almost like an out-of-body experience. Normality had to continue, regular work days, daily home chores, and the things we all inevitably have to do. But I had basically gone into autopilot. I was just trying to stay on track and keep the week as normal as possible. What happened that night and what was to come this weekend still lingered in the back of my mind, but that's where it needed to stay.

Even if I did have something connected it didn't mean I could just drop everything. Shit happens, to a lot of people, but life continues. The world doesn't stop spinning just because your head's spinning with it.

It was a strange feeling though, having this sense for something unknown and then making even the slightest discovery. Was this how the scientists I used to work with felt? When they made a discovery but didn't actually know what happened during the experiment to cause the discovery or when it happened? It just happened and now they had something new to figure out. That felt like a strange connection to make, but I couldn't help it. I hadn't worked with those people in years but the relevance just popped into my mind when I thought about it.

Thankfully, Wes always had some project car he was working on, so that would be keeping him busy this weekend. That wasn't even out of the norm for him, I knew it would be happening because it happened every weekend. I didn't even have to ask.

His cars normally took up at least a few hours out of each weekend, if not a whole day. And for now, until we were able to afford our first house, those projects were all kept at his parents.

Wow… I never thought I'd be saying I was grateful for all his project cars. This ghost stuff really was getting to me.

I didn't hate his project cars. I wasn't exactly jumping up and down with excitement every time he showed me a new one he wanted, but I didn't hate them. It would just be nice if some of them were a tad bit more functional. Or, if he, in the very least, wanted to have a more decent option to use for his daily car. But he didn't care as much about that, as long as it gave him what he needed and got him from point A to point B. Otherwise, he wanted fun cars, which I understood to an extent. He was the epitome of a car guy. What only confused me is that currently none of the 'fun' cars were actually usable...at all. None.

But, it's always been a passion for him and it keeps him busy.

Plus, now having somehow made it through this last week, this hobby of his was about to grant me the alone time tomorrow I desperately needed.

I don't know why this felt so secretive. It wasn't that I meant to keep anything hidden, I just needed a little bit more time before I said anything. I didn't want any bad reaction and what kind of reaction could I expect from him when I didn't even know how to react myself yet. I felt like I sounded crazy. It does sound crazy! If you weren't there, who would believe something like that? Sure, I have a video but skeptics are skeptics.

Wes explained everything with science. Of course, I obviously trusted science too and looked through the same lens to explain most things. But this, this you couldn't explain away. Not yet anyway.

I just needed it to stay mine a little longer.

I'd attempted some similar experimentation with Maia during the past year, but this time was different. This hadn't felt like a stranger was in my home. It didn't feel foreign. It felt like it knew me. But how? Had I seen it in a dream before? Even that was too abstract for how close it felt. But, it didn't feel like someone I'd known in life either. I don't think whoever or whatever this was had ever been alive. It felt almost like when you get a little older and run into your parents' old friends who haven't seen you since you were a toddler. You don't remember them at all, but they're telling you they've known you your whole life.

I didn't by any means believe tomorrow's experiment would answer all my questions. Hell, at this point, I wondered if it would answer any. It could end up leaving me with even more, if that was even possible. And if I was being completely honest, I wasn't sure I wanted all the answers.

The real question was, would it even happen again? Did the strange energy leave already? Maybe I'd connect with someone else entirely. Now that would be interesting. But if that happened...Why? Out of everyone, why me? Could I have some deeper connection?

Ugh, dammit, I was letting it get to my head again. I couldn't do that today. Wes would be home soon and I had plans for tonight. I needed to focus on that.

I slapped the side of my head as if I could knock the thoughts right out of it. Now was not the time.

I'd been holding it together pretty well all week, considering. I'd been anxious, but I'd at least been able to keep myself from having a full blown breakdown, telling Wes about everything, drowning myself in a rabbit hole of research, or even doing a full blown seance in the living room, but it was still sitting in my brain stewing.

Now I just needed to breathe. Keep myself calm for one more day, one more night. Tonight was not for any spirit or ugly bad energy. Tonight was already planned and it was planned for Wes and I.

As much as I'd tried to hide it, he'd been able to tell something was off with me this week. He could tell I was distracted. I tried writing it off as just being tired. The apartment stayed clean, we were both eating healthy, and I was working. I may not have seemed really happy a hundred percent of the time, but I was being really productive. I, at least, thought I was hiding it well.

For Wes, he's glad to see me doing things and making sure I'm taking care of myself, even when I seem off. But, being super productive isn't as big of a deal when I don't seem happy. Normally he would be telling me to switch things up right now if he thought things were too off. So tonight would be the breather. Tonight was for us both to relax and forget about everything but the two of us.

I just had to keep reminding myself that with a cleared mind I always learned and found out exactly what I wanted to know.

With everything going on, I was determined to make tonight a bit extra special. Wes would be home soon and I had filled the day with chores just to prep and ensure tonight would go as planned. And to keep my mind focused after this morning's brain rant.

The living room was already set up and ready for dinner to be served, though it would first start with snacks as we waited for dinner to finish.

For dinner, I had the perfect recipe that was just waiting to be put to good use. It was one of both of our favorites. Though, this time cooking it would also be partially a hopeful experiment. I'd only cooked it once before and that was with my dad when he was first teaching it to me. That was about a year ago now and this would be my second attempt.

At least the first time turned out really good!

It was expensive enough to make that we usually only had it about once or twice a year. But, tonight's occasion just felt like a good enough reason to go all out. Though it also took about 4 hours to cook and I normally make dinners that take no longer than an hour.

I'm not patient when it comes to cooking.

I like to cook and I like food. But I don't like waiting when I'm hungry...

So I'd made sure to put dinner in the oven a couple hours before he would be home. We may not be eating dinner right away, but I wanted that familiar smell to be filling the room when he walked in the door.

"Hey! It smells great in here, what is all this?" Wes said finally walking through the door and setting his stuff down.

I had also cleaned the whole apartment, lit the candles, prepped and set up snacks, and I even set out our table top fireplace. I really had decided to go all out for our spontaneous date night in. But it felt right. We rarely do these things with how busy life has been lately. We're just happy to sit and relax at the end of the day when we have the last few hours together. But tonight, when I wasn't sure what to expect out of tomorrow, I opted for a bit more.

"We haven't really had a date night in a while and it's been such a long week for both of us, I thought we'd do something a little extra tonight." I said, coming to greet him while he took his shoes off, "I even have dessert!" I raised my eyebrows like he should be extra impressed.

"This all looks and sounds great babe." He kicked off his shoes and gave me a quick kiss, "I'm just going to change real fast and I'll be right out."

He'd finally gotten out of the car industry a few months ago, when he'd come home dirty with grease from working on cars all day. But he was still used to and preferred changing almost as soon as he was through the door.

"No problem, I'm finishing setting up and we can pick what to watch."

Finally, nothing felt heavy tonight. This was exactly what I needed. A night with Wes to just enjoy food and each other.

In that moment I realized just how much I really did need this. Seeing him just as happy at what I put together, just for the night together, my stress melted away. There could be no dark energy in this room, at least not right now.

"Are there any new videos from those guys out yet?" He was talking about the ghost hunters we liked to watch.

"No." I said, maybe too quickly, "I...I think we have a few more weeks until their next one." I hadn't looked to confirm, I just wanted to move on.

"Oh, ok yea, I guess it hasn't been quite a month yet." He was already walking toward the bedroom.

Thank God.

No ghosts tonight, no stress, just food, Wes, and a fun movie.

"I already have something picked out anyway!" I called down the hall.

He'd been suggesting this one for weeks. He knew I wanted to watch it, though I'd been refusing for a while now. It's a long story, too long to get into the details now.

It was a musical and depending on the musical I really didn't mind them. There were some I really loved. But he hated musicals and I was also trying not to subject him to that. I figured when I finally came around to letting myself watch the movie I would just enjoy it on my own. But this one, he actually showed interest in and because he knew I had kind of secretly been wanting to see it, he would watch it with me.

I feel like it might be because of all the movies and shows I watched with him for him, but it was still very sweet when he made the gesture.

I flipped on the TV, he was still in the bedroom changing from his work clothes, and I pulled up the movie. I ran over to the kitchen to grab the snack tray and some plates in case we found them necessary. The perfect movie night setup. I was very satisfied with myself.

We really hadn't had a proper movie night or date night in so long. Life had gotten so busy. We were both working a lot and recently we realized we were starting to let work take over our lives rather than just be a part of life. Not even allowing ourselves to have hobbies.

We're both really creative people and we needed hobbies outside of work. Otherwise, burnout was a much faster turnaround. Though neither of us really had much for hobbies before, other than his car projects obviously, I think this recent realization was the kickstart we both needed. But of course, hobbies on top of work, if you don't find one together right away, makes life even busier.

So tonight was no work, no hobbies, no outside distractions, just us. Maybe we'd find something soon that we could both enjoy, use to make date days or nights a little more frequent. But for now, we had tonight.

"You pick something?" Wes rounded the hall corner to the living room, pulling down the remainder of the shirt he had just changed. A simple black T-shirt, as always.

"I decided to finally give it a shot. Felt like a good night for it." I pointed at the screen to show the Wicked cover displayed.

"Oh! Ok, sure, let's do it." He had a big smile on his face, looking from the TV down to the tray of snacks I'd laid out. For now, chips, salsa, queso, cheese, crackers, and of course, popcorn.

"Here, sit, I'll grab us drinks." I was still standing over the tray, having just finished setting up.

"I'll do some iced tea, please."

Neither of us had really been drinking anymore. We did once in a while, but really only if we went out or if it was a special occasion with friends or family. With just the two of us, we didn't really care for it anymore. Plus, I really hated the nasty headache I'd get from even a slight buzz.

I returned with his iced tea and a water for myself. Plopping down beside him on the couch.

"Ok, hopefully it's as good as everyone's been saying." I said as I hit play, "I haven't heard a single bad review. Oh, and dinner should be ready in about an hour."

"What's dinner?" Wes was grabbing a handful of chips.

"It's a surprise," I smiled at him. I couldn't remember the last time we'd even had this meal.

Tonight was perfect. Our stomachs were full with chips and dip, corned beef, and chocolate fondue for dessert. A little something extra I had decided would be the perfect addition. It was. I don't remember the last time I had fondue, but I never forget how much I love it. Although now I felt like I needed to be rolled to bed.

The movie was just as good as I expected. I'd even cried at the part everyone else had talked about crying at. I swear I've become such a crybaby the older I've gotten. It is so easy to make me cry with movies, TV, and books now it's ridiculous. I just get too invested if it's a good story.

I cried at a commercial the other day and knew I'd officially started turning into my mother.

Tonight felt good though. Neither of us were ready to get up once the movie was over. Too tired, too full, for a moment I thought we both may just fall asleep on the couch. For the first time all week what I needed to do tomorrow was not even on my mind.

I noticed Wes glance over at me though I didn't fully look back at him. I was too busy willing myself to get up but my will and body were both failing me and I was just sinking farther into the couch. It took him that single glance to push himself off the couch and start clearing the dishes.

"I've got this stuff, you go get ready for bed." He said, focusing on the dishes.

"You don't have to, I can help." I tried to argue, but I was still building that will to even move. I was not winning that battle with my body.

He paused gathering and chuckled, "You're good, I've got this, thank you for tonight." He leaned down for a light kiss, "Plus, you don't look like you'd make it to the kitchen carrying any of these dishes." He had a sarcastic grin but just turned back to gathering plates.

"Well, thank you," I said with a slight glare at the comment.

But that will I had been trying to find now seemed to be completely gone.

I woke up hours later, still on the couch, with a blanket laid over me and the lights off other than a dim lamp in the corner. Bambi was laying next to me but Wes had definitely gone to bed. Leaving that dim light just in case I woke up and wanted to come to bed.

I picked up my phone, more out of habit than really thinking I missed any notifications. I had crashed. It was

2AM and the realization of what was to come today came flooding back.

"Ugh. I can do this. It'll be fine." The mix of emotions and nervousness was actually annoying me. Tonight had gone so well and I was feeling so good, "I just need to know something from all this. Anything."

I was just talking to myself in the quiet, dark room.

The more I let it get to me, the more I was letting the fear take over. The more I was letting it win.

Pulling myself off the couch, I went and washed my face. I would start my research after Wes left this morning. Then I could get things started this afternoon. I had no other plans and he would be gone all day. It had to be today.

I decided to take a hot shower to try and let the steam help release some of the returning tension. I don't know how long I was in there, I just know I let the water start to get cold before I got out.

My phone buzzed on the office desk, it was Maia already, "Ready for today?" 2:30 AM for me, 5:30 AM for her, and it was Saturday. She was more ready than me.

Obviously, SHE wasn't the one doing anything. She just got to be the audience from afar. Lucky little witch.

I shoved down my annoyance though, she was all I had in this right now, "No, but today's the day. I'll text you in a bit but send me anything else you've found."

Chapter 4

I woke up minutes before my alarm was set to go off. My body was so used to my sleep schedule by now, this had become a normal habit. Wes, per usual, remained dead to the world.

Maybe at this point the alarm was more of a placebo, but whatever worked to trick my brain worked for me, and my body knew it was time. I just needed that morning me time.

If I did end up sleeping through it on the weekend, Wes would just roll over and silence it himself. He didn't even bother waking me up. If I didn't wake up and hadn't told him otherwise, he'd assume I left it set by mistake.

I slipped out of bed and quietly pulled on my robe, doing my best not to wake him.

By no means have I ever been a morning person. I've actually always been more of a night owl. I just learned that I simply liked being awake during the dark hours when it felt like the world was still asleep. It felt peaceful.

For Wes, he set an alarm when he needed it and when he needed it, he set fifteen. If he didn't have an alarm set, and didn't ask me to wake him up, I let him sleep as late as he wanted.

Plus, I had no problem with the extra time to myself in the morning. Coffee in hand, reading my book, I wasn't complaining. Especially not today.

A little added time to clear my head was nothing but positive.

"Ok, I'm finally waking up and having my coffee. Wes is still asleep, I'm not sure yet when he'll be leaving this morning." My quick update to Maia.

"Do you have everything?"

God, she was fast.

"Almost. I still have to go grab a couple things once he leaves." Earlier this week she'd sent me a list of what I needed from the store for today. She didn't, however, bother to include any explanation, just the items. "How does this stuff work anyway?"

The list included a couple crystals that, according to her, could not wait and I needed to buy them immediately to prepare. Just having them with me would be enough but they needed to be charged under the moonlight first.

Luckily, these types of things weren't necessarily uncommon in my area. Not for paranormal use but just in general, a lot of one-with-nature type of people around here.

I'd done what I was told, gotten the crystals early, and set them out on the balcony two nights ago to get as much moonlight as possible. Now they sat locked away in the cold, dark drawer of my nightstand until I was ready for them.

Wes hadn't noticed a thing, precisely what I had intended.

"What'd you mean? Did you get the crystals? You just need to keep them with you."

"Yes, I got the crystals, I got them both charged. I mean, like, the herbs and stuff. Am I supposed to eat anything? Put something in the doors and windows? Build a circle around the flashlight?" I honestly didn't know but none of it would've surprised me at this point.

"You're not casting some spell over crushed herbs or drinking a brew from your cauldron if that's what you're asking."

A bit snarky.

"Well, what the hell am I doing?" I didn't think either of those things, but I also didn't think the point of herbs was to just be scattered around the room in plastic grocery bags. Was the spirit just going to get scared by the idea that I'm some hoarder and leave?

"Ok, ok, well you have the black tourmaline and amethyst charged, so that's set. Good. You need to keep them with you."

"Ok, so in my pocket? Holding them? Do they just need to be in the room I'm in?"

"Keep the tourmaline in your pocket. You'll probably just want to hold the amethyst. The black tourmaline is for protection against negative energy. The amethyst is to help create better connection."

I was honestly really intrigued by her list. She had really gotten into crystals this last year, even sent me a book specifically about them. But I knew they were going to be her first go-to when I asked her to start researching for me.

I watched my phone, waiting for her to continue, now onto the herbs.

"When you go to the store, make sure you get everything I mentioned. The chamomile, you're going to separate and put into a few different bowls. Put one in each room to ward off bad energy from entering.

"Get a little pouch, if you don't already have one, and use that for the lavender to keep for yourself. That also wards bad energy and will surround yourself. Kind of double duty with the black tourmaline.

"Last, but absolutely not least, the sage. I know you already know, but obviously, burn the sage all throughout your place when you're done. For the final cleanse."

She sent each chunk as a separate message, emphasizing each step of instruction.

She had certainly done the research she'd promised, "Damn. You know, you really are starting to sound kind of witchy now." I responded to her flood of instructions. "I'm thankful for your spells, Madam Maia." Now I was just laughing to myself.

I had to find the humor somewhere in all of this.

"You know...I don't mind the sound of that. Has a ring to it." I could hear the grin at her new title through the message.

"I'm going to see if there's any history I can find out about my apartment or neighborhood." I needed to come up with some additional questions in case it passed the initail round.

God, what was I? Initial round? As true as the sentiment may be, I cringed at my own thought.

"If it does come back, it is possible it could just be a trapped angry spirit or something like that."

"At this point, one could only hope." Maia sounded about as hopeful as I felt.

Whoever or whatever this was came from somewhere. I knew my first questions. My first questions would tell me a lot. But, if I'm wrong and it actually passed that first test, there were only two options left. I would either be connecting with an entirely different spirit, or I was wrong.

I didn't mind the former, the latter I wasn't sure what to do with. It was also still too early and I lacked the caffeine necessary to process the hours ahead.

Instead, assuming I had a few hours before Wes woke up, I downed the rest of my coffee and dove into my own research.

I was so zoned in on the computer, I didn't even notice Wes wake up.

I would normally hear the bedroom door open, his footsteps passing in the hall, or catch a glimpse through the cracked office door. But I was locked in.

This stuff was so interesting I couldn't help it. Not just the paranormal aspect, I was obsessed with history in general. It always felt like untold mysteries were locked away in little snippets of information. I could easily fall down any rabbit hole.

My eyes snapped off the screen only when Wes' foot thudded against the office door.

"Good morrrrning!" He always used a goofy greeting in the morning, especially when he saw me deeply concentrated on something.

Cold brew in hand, he came over to the side of the desk and picked something to fidget with. He rarely drank regular coffee anymore, typically Celsius, or cold brew if it was the last option.

"Whaaaaat're you doing?"

I had clicked out of my main tabs and gone into my email when he walked in. Because why would I be looking into the history of our complex and neighborhood?

"Oh, uh, I was just checking in on emails. I ordered some things, seeing when they should be here. After finishing some morning reading." I held up my Kindle. That was easy enough and I really had recently ordered some new clothes. Packages would be arriving soon. "You sleep ok?"

"Yeah, thanks for letting me sleep in. The time change this week has been rough. I didn't even think about it before but I think that's the reason I've been so tired lately."

"Yea, of course. You clearly needed it." I tapped my phone to check the time, "How early were you planning to leave this morning?"

"I really want to get a few things done, so I think I'm just going to get an early start." He usually felt a little guilty leaving early on Saturdays since we'd get less or no time together. "Probably take a quick shower and get going."

"Ok, don't worry about it. I have some things to get done today and some quick errands to run when you head out." I was really trying to reassure him.

"I'm sorry I won't be around much today."

"It's ok, really. We still have tomorrow." I smiled and reached to touch his arm.

The longer he was gone today the easier everything would be for me.

Part of me still hoped one day he might be as into this stuff as me. Watching the videos together was one thing, sharing the experience was something entirely different.

"Yes, we will definitely have our time tomorrow." He leaned down to kiss me, "Ok, I'm going to take a shower."

I really didn't go out much. The driving, the crowds, the parking, it all stressed me out too much when too many people were out. If I did go anywhere it was saved for a weekday when I wasn't as busy, and reserved for the morning.

Sometimes I'd forget why I didn't go out much and think I wanted to, but as soon as I'd venture out again, I was always quickly reminded why I never did. Especially on the weekends.

Currently, I only had one exception. One little grocery store down the street that had a completely different vibe from anywhere else in our busy little area. I never minded making a trip.

No matter the day, unless it was maybe a holiday, it was rarely busy, especially not this early. That's where I was headed this morning.

After today, depending on how everything went, I knew I'd need to find a proper store for supplies. But this was quick. I started with the easiest, fastest, and most hopeful option first. It also may have helped make me feel a bit more sane.

If I'd gone to a proper specialty store, I knew I would have let myself get sucked in to the wonder and intrigue. I'd just end up coming home with much more than I needed.

As long as the grocery store had what I needed, that was more than sufficient for today's plans.

"I probably looked like I was there for a drug deal or something, but I got it all. I'm starting on the prep now" I texted Maia when I'd made it back to the apartment, shopping bag in hand. Wes had already left before I had gone to the store.

The store, shockingly, had everything Maia listed—lavender, chamomile, sage. I knew I had looked sketchy, hunched over baskets of herbs at 9AM and avoiding eye contact like the plague or as if I was involved in something illicit. But, it's fine, I got what I needed.

Bambi was now investigating the bag I'd set on the floor, unsure of the new smells.

Instead of just responding, Maia called me laughing, "What'd you mean you looked like you were there for a drug deal? That was fast though, I didn't think one of those shops would be open so early."

"They weren't open this early, I tried the grocery store first, it was all there!" I had answered knowing she was only calling because she was laughing and confused by my comment.

"But, yes, I definitely looked like I was there for a drop or something." I was chuckling at myself, wiping a hand down my own shameful face. "It's still early, I'm in my hoodie, keeping my head down, and I'm just endlessly browsing for random herbs. Then I was too self-conscious and felt like everyone was looking at me so that made me keep glancing around at everyone else. I'm pretty sure it looked like I was already on something or there to get more of whatever I was already on."

She was laughing even harder now.

"Just your average person trying to get some random herbs at 9 AM!"

"Oh my God." Was all she got out, "Ok, well are you home now?"

"Yes, thank God. I'm home and I'm about to start putting everything together."

"Ok, well let me know when you're done." We both hung up.

Bringing my attention back to the bag, Bambi was looking at me as if whatever inside were new treats for her. Now I felt bad, I normally did bring something home for her so I couldn't just ignore it. I'd been trying to get in and out of the store so fast I hadn't thought to even grab something for her.

She couldn't exactly have one of the herbs though so I gave her one of her normal treats as an apology and began preparations.

Four bowls for the chamomile, a bowl for each room. The kitchen, dining, and living room were technically one big room, but, for precaution I decided two bowls would be best. One bowl for the bedroom, and one to put in the office after.

I already had a small pouch so I had opted not to get a new one at the store. I grabbed the one I had set aside and added the lavender to that, tightening the straps and sliding my wrist through the loops. The perfect little protection bracelet.

Then there was the sage. That didn't need a bowl or a pouch, I just needed my lighter. I set both as a pair on the counter for now.

I needed to set up the chamomile.

One bowl on the kitchen counter, one in the living room, leaving it on the shelf that acted as a mantle. I set one in the bedroom on the dresser, it was close to the door and the most central part of the room. The last would be in the office. I didn't have too much room, but just enough space on the small shelf behind my desk. But, for now, it would go in the connected bathroom so I could simply move it in after.

Ok, everything was almost ready.

I took the sage and lighter back to the office, placing it on the desk just to be ready. Last but not least, the crystals.

"Are you ready?" It had only taken me about 10 minutes to prepare and place everything before responding back to Maia.

"Are you?" Her response.

I honestly didn't know, "I don't really have a choice." I had one final step but my feet wouldn't move. "Everything is set up, I just need to get the crystals and take out the flashlight."

"Do you want me on the phone?"

I really thought about that question. It felt comforting to have someone there, but if she was on the phone I wasn't going to be able to record anything.

If I blacked out because I was overwhelmed or if something happened, what if I didn't remember? What if something happened and I actually needed to show Maia? I couldn't do this on the phone.

"I need to be able to record..." I had to do this on my own, "It'll be fine, that's what all this stuff is for."

I took a breath. The crystals didn't start anything, they were just the last part I needed to set up.

Finally, my body gave in and I made my way to the nightstand. Slowly opening the drawer to reveal the two crystals waiting inside. They looked like they hadn't just charged in the moonlight but rather locked a piece of the moon itself inside each one.

I took the tourmaline and put it in my back pocket as Maia had recommended and simply kept hold of the amethyst. I had debated also having a small bag for this one but if it's supposed to help with connection I assumed it may work better with direct skin contact.

Suddenly, I felt my whole body release a bit of tension. My breathing began to calm. My heartbeat slowed.

Everything was ready back in the office and now I finally felt ready too. Probably a placebo, similar to my alarm, but hey if it worked, it worked.

I had thought about getting candles. I could dim the lights in the office and do this by candle light. But my office was the only room that had a street facing window. It may be my own paranoia but even just the thought of anyone outside seeing a light going on and off in my office made me feel self conscious.

I wasn't sure if it would be obvious, especially at this time of day, or if anyone would even be able to see it. But, either way, I didn't want to risk it. The main light remained on, no candles.

Ok, no more procrastinating, it was time.

Back in the office I had my notebook, every single question listed. I would not forget anything. Anything that became unnecessary could be left out, but I would not unintentionally leave out a question because of my terrible memory.

I let out a slow breath. My questions were waiting to be answered and that flashlight was waiting to answer them.

A chill went straight up my arm as I pulled the flashlight from the drawer. Almost like a presence had already entered the room and was ready to speak. It froze me in place for a split second before I turned and knelt to the floor.

Already I felt eyes on me that weren't in the room.

"Ok, I'm about to begin, I'll get back to you when I have an update." I sent Maia one last message before getting started.

"Good luck!"

I propped my phone where it would be able to see the flashlight if it turned on or off, ready to record. Setting up the flashlight, I faced it away from me on the ground. My hands were shaking to the point I was barely able to tap the phone to record.

I took one last very deep breath and began, "Is anyone there that would like to speak with me?"

It didn't even take ten seconds, the flashlight snapped on.

Shit.

Chapter 5

It was here. All that time wondering if it would show up again today and I don't think it ever left.

A week of preparation. A week of wondering. Hoping that it still would so I could get answers, but also slightly hoping it wouldn't. Yet, all I could do now was stare at the flashlight in disbelief. It turned on so fast this time, even faster than before. But last time, it had turned on to answer my question and immediately turned back off. Now, the light hadn't even dimmed. It was waiting for me. Waiting for the next question or request.

"Can you turn the light off now?" My brows raised, unable to look away. It turned off almost immediately.

I hadn't realized I'd been holding most of my breath until I let out a full sigh the moment the light switched off. That was only the first question and it was barely even a question. All I wanted was to confirm something or someone was here.

I looked around the room, as if I'd catch a glimpse or shadow of whoever was with me.

Of course I wouldn't.

The whole time, just as it had remained on, the flashlight stayed off now, again, waiting.

I forced my focus back. I had my protections in place and so far nothing was trying to harm me.

"Was I speaking with you the other night?" I continued, finally building back the courage to ask the next question, "If it was, can you turn the flashlight back on?" On.

Ok, ok. So that's confirming this is the same connection I'd made before. It made sense with the feeling I was getting and how fast the light was reacting. But who was this? Where did it come from? How did it get here? Why was it here?

My hands were starting to shake over my notes. I had so many questions that needed answers. Some answers I still struggled with wanting to know. The room felt so still and quiet, just me and the flashlight.

It was still earlier in the afternoon but I could barely hear the cars driving by outside. I couldn't focus on anything outside of this room. Staring at my notes, deciding on my next question.

I had completely forgotten that my phone was still setup to record. I had no idea how long it had been going for, if it was even still recording that is. But, I couldn't just have footage of myself contemplating and stressing, using up all the storage for nothing. Grabbing my phone, I hit stop.

Ten minutes had already gone by. No idea how I was able to record that much.

I couldn't take much time, but I could at least quickly edit this first clip. All I had to do was shorten it, cutting out everything at the end that had nothing but silence. I'd barely asked two questions and then basically froze.

I re-set the phone propped up, I could worry about updating Maia in a minute. I didn't have enough time to worry about that yet. I'd already wasted too much time frozen, thinking, contemplating.

"Are you still here? Are you still with me?" I put the question out into the room. The light flashed on. This time a chill went straight down my spine. It was waiting for me. Being patient with me?

My head tilted and brows narrowed, "Did I know you in life? When you were alive?"

Nothing.

"Is that a no or do you not want to answer?" Well that was technically two questions I guess.

"Do you know me?" On.

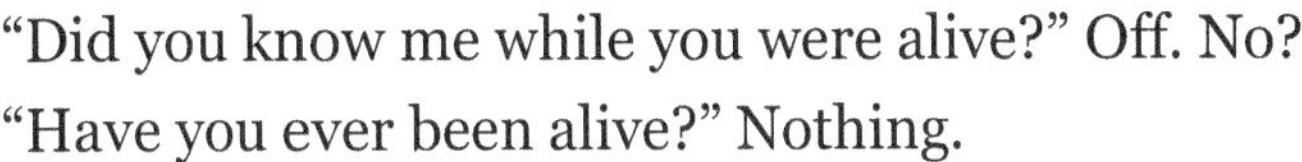

"Did you know me while you were alive?" Off. No?

"Have you ever been alive?" Nothing.

Nothing was my answer.

But suddenly, the light snapped on.

"So you have been?" I just stared while it remained on...but then it seemed to dim... I narrowed my eyes watching, counting down in my head...3...2...1, off, on. What was happening?

I had written down the question expecting to catch any negative energy in a lie. I needed to know if it would tell me if it knew me from life as a friend or family. That would make it easier. That was the first test. The historical information I had looked into earlier was in case it had passed and didn't tell me it knew me. With that information, I could still try to figure out who it was.

I hadn't really thought about what I'd do had it failed, but also passed the fail...How does it pass and fail at the same time?

Negative entities lie, they pretend to be someone they aren't. Whoever this was just wasn't answering, but then they were. I didn't know what was happening.

There was another test for negative energy but we weren't even close to there yet.

I took a breath and asked again, "Did you know me when you were alive?" It snapped and remained off.

There was suddenly a very strange feeling in the room, a glaring energy. The calm had drained from the room. I felt crowded, nearly claustrophobic.

"Ok, you didn't know me. Have you ever been alive?" The light remained off for a few moments. Then, slowly, almost like it was hesitant or fighting for it, it turned back on. So slowly I almost thought I saw the flashlight itself start to move as it finally fully lit the spot on the wall it faced. But just as soon as the light reached its full potential, it snuffed out like a candle being blown out.

My notes were rested in my lap. I wasn't sure what to think. Had it? Had it not? Did it not know? Did it not want to tell me?

"Do you know that you're dead?"

Nothing.

God, I wish I could ask more than these simple yes or no questions. But it's fine. That's why I came prepared. I may have gotten a little off track but I could bring this back.

I had to think. All I had was that it was the same thing I'd connected with earlier this week, it didn't know me but may have been alive at some point. But it didn't know that it was dead.

My heart started racing. It clearly knew what I was trying to do with some of these questions and was trying to confuse me. Could it still be someone who's just angry and trapped?

"Can you come and go from here as you wish?" The light came back on. My breath caught. I was not expecting that answer. Then why was it here?

"Is there something here that you want?"

On again!

So it's not trapped…Unresolved business?

Before I could keep going, I really needed to ask the biggest questions. I almost didn't want to. I knew if I got the answers I didn't want I would have to stop everything. I didn't want to stop yet, I needed to know more.

My phone was still recording. I don't know how it kept going for so long. Normally, anytime I tried recording it only went as long as two or three minutes before I'd get a warning about storage. I reached over, clicked off the recording and practically tossed it back to the ground.

There was something here that it wanted. What did that mean? Why would you want something here when you're already dead? Did it used to live here? Was this a spirit who had been murdered and maybe they wanted justice? This was specifically a situation I had been looking for earlier today but there was no record for the area.

I wasn't going to get anywhere until I asked these next two questions though. The determining questions.

My palms were sweating now, making the amethyst slightly harder to keep hold of. I leaned forward to grab the tourmaline out of my back pocket. It was good in there but felt better in my hand. This was all a chance. The air felt so heavy suddenly, it was like they knew what I was about to ask.

I kept my voice steady, with all the confidence I could bring into it, "Are you here with negative intentions?"

The light gave nothing. Not even a flicker this time. But it didn't feel like a no. It was avoiding.

Then the flicker came again! Another flicker of light after a long silence, quickly snuffed. So fast that this time I nearly missed the flash. If you weren't looking at the light you may have missed it.

My eyes darted from the spot on the wall it had lit up back to the flashlight. Then it hit me, "Is there more than one person here trying to speak to me?"

Another flicker.

It was almost like whatever energy was here was trying to stop the other.

"Got it. Ok." I had to think. For now I just had to go with it, "Negative energy of any kind is not welcome here! You are not welcome to speak to me, touch me, attach, follow, or stay here. You need to leave. Our conversation is over."

I didn't even realize I shut my eyes while making the demand until after I said it. Looking around the room everything had gone still, the air suddenly lighter. I let out the breath that had tightened in my chest. But something still felt off though. The flashlight had turned off when I cut contact, but now, looking around, surveying the room, I looked up. The main light on the ceiling had also gone out. The switch on the wall by the door had been flipped off.

All I could do was sit in silence. Staring at the flashlight that, just moments ago, had been so active. My hands, a crystal still in each one, fell completely limp in my lap, yet still clung to those crystals.

There was nothing different about the room, there had been nothing different. I hadn't done anything to this room other than put the flashlight on the ground. Any protection precautions I'd taken were in other rooms and on me personally. But I knew the room had felt different. Not now, but during the connection.

I felt connected. I can't even fully explain it. It was gone now. Did the stone work that well? It almost felt like I had this sort of reach, but with my mind. Like I could extend a tether to another side. But it was also blocked and hindered. Was that because of this strange energy that kept connecting?

Wait—I snapped slightly out of the weird trance I'd fallen into. There was someone else here...Someone else had tried to come through. But that energy, that spirit, that entity, that whatever-it-was, was trying to stop it. It had stopped it. When it was fully trying to answer me was when everything went out...

What was happening? What did it want? What was trying to connect? How was this all even working so well?

My phone buzzed, snapping me fully back to reality. Maia had flooded my phone. Understandably, I didn't even realize it had already been thirty minutes.

It felt like hours could've passed and only minutes had passed at the same time.

"What the hell is going on? Are you ok?" Each message was about a minute apart "Who do I even call if something goes wrong? How do I even know if something is going wrong? We didn't really discuss or think about that!"

She had a point.

But her messages continued, "The police? A priest? Exorcist?" Options... She was at least thinking about the options, "I don't even know who for the last two!"

Ok, now I could tell she was ranting out loud to herself too.

"Hey! Sorry! I'm ok. But that was wild." I filled her in on everything. I hadn't even left my spot on the floor yet, I'd barely had a moment to breathe, let alone move.

"Wow... What does that mean?" She finally said.

Once I'd finally sent my response she'd called.

"I have no idea. But it felt weird. There was someone else here. I know the original thing wasn't good, I just don't know how bad it is. And I'm not really sure what to do now or what to do next." I was kind of spitting out word vomit, just saying what was circling in my mind. I couldn't formulate any real thoughts or solutions from this information yet.

"Have you cleansed yet?"

That part... I had actually completely forgotten about.

"I haven't. I'm still on the floor with the light. I haven't even tried the light switch again." Figured I should at least make sure it also still worked. "But...but do you think I still should?" I was starting to think now.

"What do you mean, should you still cleanse?" Maia was appalled, expected.

"Well, obviously I was going to. But now, it's more than just one. Maybe there's more."

"So you don't want to do the cleanse now?"

"Before it was just to get rid of the negative energy. Now if there's more and they aren't all bad, what if it gets rid of everything?" I was trying to think of what else I could do now.

"I don't know. I get it, but that feels risky."

"Of course it's risky." I was matter of fact, tossing my hands. I talked with my hands in general but it got worse when I was frustrated or anxious.

"I don't have a lot of other choices though." I paused, I was starting to get an idea, "But, what if I don't need it for now?" I could feel her eyes narrow through the phone.

"Everything stayed where it was supposed to. What if I just kept the chamomile where it is? I could go get some more lavender, get a few more little pouches and scatter them in spots. Leave it confined somewhere if it chooses to return.”

“Ok, I don’t like it, but that is a thought.” There was something else she didn’t want to say, “Ok, I mean, I was going to tell you to do something like that as precaution for the next, probably week anyway.”

“HA, ok! See, I need to know what else is going on here.” Something more was happening. I kept feeling something more. The crystals were supposed to add protection but I didn’t think I was supposed to actually feel anything holding them, any sensations. My hands were still tingling.

That much I hadn’t mentioned yet to Maia.

“Wait, do those also work in the form of say, a candle? Could I burn a couple candles? I feel like that would enhance it but it could be the opposite.”

“Oh, why didn’t I think of that! Yes! Get candles! That’s even better.”

“Well at least I still have time before Wes should be home. Now I need to go find those.”

I was finally starting to get up, I still hadn’t gotten off the office floor. But, there was a game plan now. “Oh shit.” I grabbed the desk and nearly dropped the phone.

“What! What now?” Maia demanded.

“Oh stop, nothing. Nothing. I just finally stood up and my foot’s asleep.” I started laughing.

"You've still been on the floor this whole time?" She sounded shocked. "Wait, did you get anything recorded?" Like she had just remembered that was part of the whole plan.

I mean I had completely forgotten too. Everything had gotten so off track, I was trying to record questions but it all went so left field.

"Oh my God, sorry, yeah. I just left it on record. I was going to cut it up where it made sense and send you the clips." I switched over to speaker phone. "Let me see if I can just do it while you're still on the phone, I have you on speaker."

I had hit record and stop once, that clip was there. I had hit record one more time and stopped just before my last questions. But there was no second clip. There was nothing else. One clip of the flashlight turning on and off, my voice in the background. Everything else was gone.

"It's gone Maia." I was staring, blinking at my phone like I had to be missing it somehow, like my eyes were tricking me.

"What do you mean, gone?"

I hit send on the only remaining clip I had. "I mean, I recorded everything. I sent you the first thing I got, everything else is gone."

Chapter 6

It all worked. Worked even better than we were expecting. Better than we probably wanted, honestly. But how could the recording just be gone?

"Is it at all possible that you thought you hit record but didn't? Or maybe you accidentally deleted it?" Maia was trying to rationalize it. Find some reason to explain how that second recording could simply vanish. As if it never existed. It made no sense.

I was trying to hold myself together and not freak out.

"No, absolutely not." I was standing firm. I know what I did. I know what I saw. I just don't know what happened.

I wasn't doing very well at the holding myself together part.

"I saw the recording start before I set the phone back down. I already checked my deleted folder." At this point I started swearing up a storm. If I was a nail-biter I'm sure I'd be doing that too.

Was that normal? To have anxiety to the point that you wished you had one of those typical habits associated with it? Like I wanted to self-soothe but the normal habits never worked for me.

Shopping and tattoos, that's what worked for me.

"Ok... Well what do you think could have happened?" I could tell Maia really wanted a reassuring answer. Unfortunately, I didn't have one.

"I think this is bigger than we thought. I think the situation that just happened, and whatever that was, did not want that part recorded."

It wasn't reasuring, but it was the truth.

"Well, then what now?"

"Now, I need to go find those candles." I started looking up the scents online. I had no idea where to go when you're looking for very specific scents. "Then I need to try again. But next time, you're going to be on the phone."

If the footage might be deleted anyway, we might as well say screw it and see if we can get further this way.

"We need to see if I can reach the other person who came through this time. They, at least, seemed more talkative, and more positive."

"Are you trying to do it again today?" Maia was sounding a little concerned at my tone.

"No, not today. Tomorrow, if Wes is busy again. Monday while he's at work if I need to wait."

I couldn't jump right back into anything. Not today. But tomorrow, tomorrow I could, and after that.

It took some digging, but I finally found a local shop that had what I needed. Wes wouldn't be home for another couple of hours; hopefully that would be enough time. The shop was thankfully pretty close so it shouldn't be an issue.

As decided, I didn't complete the final cleanse. We could figure that out later if we really had to. I needed to at least attempt confining whatever may come back first. Part of me wondered if I could still connect with anything in the safe zones. That's what I was calling the rooms with the herbs. Maybe we could isolate and confine the negative spirit to the office and still have a chat with whoever else wanted to come through. Or maybe that would just be too convenient.

The local shop I'd found was close. A hidden gem I'd never even noticed. Probably more so because I was never really looking for it though. But it wasn't just another grocery store or small market. I got lucky and found an apothecary. The Salem Sisters Apothecary.

How could I not go just based off the name alone? Now I just needed to keep myself from getting too drawn in. I only needed a few things and I could always come back later.

I knew I'd be back later.

The door chimed as I walked in. The store was nowhere near what I was expecting, but in the best way. Instead of simple shelves with bottles, trays, and maybe a glass counter holding displays, this was like walking into a mystical forest indoors. A vision you'd never expect, even noticing from the street.

Two large plants stood by the entrance, next to a small flowing fountain sitting in front of the main window. It may just look relaxing or like they also sold very holistic remedies from the outside.

There were different smaller plants all over the room - the main counter, between bookshelves, along the wall, and on some shelves next to bottles of herbs. One thing I did notice was that if one was next to a bottle, it seemed to correspond with the neighboring bottled herb.

I noticed another small fountain on the counter, with stones under the running water, an apothecary book sitting open next to it. Inviting the next customer to read.

They did have the glass case counter, but it wasn't random. This one was lined with velvet, stones and crystals laid across the fabric. All on full beautiful display.

Oh yes, I definitely had to come back.

For now, first, I needed the candles, then I would get some extra lavender. If I had some extra time, I'd allow myself to browse and admire the stone collection. This place was beautiful.

A couple shelves of candles sat near the front. Probably to hit your senses as soon as you walked in. Luckily they did have little baskets next to the counter. They looked more like the dainty ones you get at a cosmetics store versus the bulky grocery store ones.

I grabbed a candle for each room and made my way across to the herb shelves.

The options they had! Not just for herbs and spices but for collecting. Bottles, pouches, simple little bags. I opted for the pouches.

Then, I spotted even more — oils and droppers. Could those help? Maybe adding drops to the herb pouches or wearing the oils myself? I was no expert on these things but would someone here think I was crazy for asking? I couldn't explain the real reason for it.

As if my thoughts summoned her, a small younger woman emerged from a back room behind the counter.

"Oh hello! I'm sorry, I didn't hear the door chime."

She was the perfect fit to be working here. Her presence almost instantly calmed me.

She looked like an earthy witch with a gothic tone. She wore a long, black linen skirt that looked to almost meet her ankles, but stopped just above. Her poet-style blouse was completed with a black corset to match the skirt. And her hair fell in loose dark waves that you could still spot small loose twigs strewn through, as if she'd just finished some gardening. A small green gem pinned a few strands back from her face. As if she had thrown it in last-minute because it kept falling out of place.

"Oh, don't worry. I've just been browsing." I waved a hand at her sorry, "The shop is beautiful! It's my first time in."

"Wonderful! Let me know if you have any questions. If we're also your first apothecary I know it can sometimes be a lot to take in." She gave me a warm, welcoming smile.

"Actually, I did have one question." I was trying to figure out how to phrase it. "You also sell crystals, so I wasn't sure if you might know anything on the more spiritual side of the herbs?" I was so hesitant.

To my relief, her eyes lit up.

"Oh yes! Are you meaning to bring in the positive energy, keeping out the negative energy type of thing?" She picked up exactly what I meant.

Thank God I was the only one in the shop right now. I never would've been able to ask with an audience.

"Yes, exactly." I pointed at her, spot on. "I'm wanting these herbs and to put them in these pouches. But you also have oils. Would adding oils to the inside or outside hurt or help?"

"Don't waste the energy or time with the oil unless it's on your own skin or burning." She was shaking her head. "Let the herbs just do their thing." But she added, "Unless you need sage or a true cleansing herb. Burn those."

I think I just found my new best friend.

"Ok, I think I'm all set then." I'd already collected the items I needed. Now placing the basket on the counter, "I was just about to take a quick look at the crystals."

"You can definitely take a look at those, but today, I have something a bit more special for you. Since it's your first time in." She finished ringing in the items. "Now, I just need to get you in the system. What's your name?"

"Oh, ok, it's Aly." I responded.

"Last name?"

"Parker." She seemed to freeze for a moment. Her hand pausing just briefly over the keyboard but quickly recovered.

"I have what will hopefully be a wonderful surprise for you."

Leaving the computer and items on the counter, her heeled ankle boots clicked as she walked around to my side. I hadn't even noticed the break in the wall leading to even more shop space.

The rest was similar to the main shop, just even more garden coming to life.

The biggest difference was what stood on the other side of the wall. A large tree, nesting into a pond like area on the floor. It was surrounded by different rocks and flowers and the whole top of the tree bloomed across the ceiling.

"This is our Witchery section." She led me in front of the tree as I was taking in the open space. "We couldn't take the tree down when this shop space was built, so we built around it." She smiled at the tree. It was definitely a treasure to the shop.

"That's incredible." I was just standing in awe. I'd never seen a store, let alone any building built around nature. I came to the right place.

"On your first visit, if you find something you like or something you just can't leave without, we also let the tree choose something for you."

What did I say about the one-with-nature types around here?

"The tree chooses something?" I was going with it, I didn't want to insult her, but I was also very confused.

"Precisely. Take a step closer. You'll see the stones and crystals in the shallow water. See what calls to you." I looked from her to the tree to the pond, then nodded and did as I was told.

"Sometimes closing your eyes can help too."

I obliged. Curious what this pull would feel like.

It took just a few moments. I tried to relax and let myself focus. Then... There it was. My eyes snapped open to spot it. That felt so quick. Half buried, half emerged, that was the only one. That one said, "Mine."

I reached for the stone.

"Interesting..." The small woman said it under her breath like she didn't want me to hear.

"That's the moonstone... We add stones every few times to keep more variety. But that one is rare. The moonstone has never chosen anyone." She was genuinely surprised and also seemed intrigued and confused.

"I...I don't have to take it. If it's rare."

"No, no, it seems it's been waiting for you."

I looked down at the stone sitting in my hand. I wasn't quite sure what to think. But she led me back to the main area.

"As something a little extra, consider this on the house. A little gift to come back for more." She pushed the bag of items toward me smiling.

"Oh my gosh, are you sure? I can absolutely pay." She held up a hand to stop me.

"I know you'll be back again."

"Well thank you, I will."

I couldn't stop thinking about that whole interaction from the moment I was back in my car. Even now, back home, the conversation still replayed in my mind as I was getting everything set up.

But, I could think later, I needed to get this done. I placed and lit the candles — chamomile in the living room, lavender in the kitchen. Chamomile felt like a great option for the bedroom, it was a soothing scent on its own without the purpose I was using it for, so it wouldn't look out of place. Then lavender in each bathroom. Those, I figured would just look like they made sense. Chamomile might look a little out of place. I left the office empty. That was the confinement room.

The apartment was already beginning to smell amazing.

I had put the bowls away and was working on the herb pouches now. Wes still wouldn't be home for probably thirty minutes. I really had pulled this off in the nick of time. We could still have a good night and I could attempt to relax.

Though that conversation was still lingering in my mind. The whole experience really.

The woman had paused at my name, as if she recognized it. But not clearly in a good or bad way. I didn't know her. I'd never met her. Now I felt bad that I didn't even get her name. I never ask someone who's working for their name, I only accept when they offer it.

I've worked places where I've been forced to give my name to customers and it was the absolute worst. Not because of complaints, I never had someone complain about me like that. It was more like they knew your name so they felt like they could demand your attention.

Barf.

Maybe it just reminded her of someone else she knew. I knew I was probably overthinking, it was all just so strange.

To distract myself I texted Maia to fill her in.

"I found the perfect little store! Got everything I needed and you'll never guess what happened."

"Hmm...You met a witch!" I rolled my eyes at her guess.

"Ha-ha, very funny. No, but it was kinda weird. The lady working gave me a free stone, but you had to feel pulled to it." This was really the only interesting part to share, "Turns out, the one that 'chose me' was a moonstone. That's never happened according to her."

"A moonstone?" Maia was interested, "Oh things just keep getting more and more interesting. But that one is a little freaky."

"Wait, what'd you mean?"

"Well a moonstone means a few different things. But for protection, it's the strongest against it. Like you almost don't need a cleanse when you have one."

"The moonstone?" My eyes had widened, that's what it was connected to? What the hell did the stone sense around me?

"Yup. Charge it tonight." Sure, why not, no biggie. Just actual protections seeking me now.

I let out an exaggerated sigh and I got back to my herbs. It wasn't necessarily a bad thing but it didn't feel great either...That stone did start feeling a bit heavier in my back pocket though. What could possibly go wrong?

I was done by the time Wes got home. It was late but it was so nice to finally see him. The pouches were hidden and the candles were lit but all he saw was a clean apartment and smelled the blend of soothing scents. Everything was normal.

For me, all of this had only started a week ago, but nothing really felt normal anymore. Nothing was even comforting, no matter the amount of stones, crystals, and herbs you used, it still didn't soothe the nerves. Seeing Wes finally walk through the door brought me back that comfort. While he was home, I didn't have to think about any of this. I had been looking forward to my time alone to try to uncover information and find answers to these new discoveries. But I'd taken that comfort for granted a little bit. When I was alone I couldn't stop thinking about these spirits we were trying to contact, the stones, the herbs, and what was happening. Now, seeing him walk through the door, the relief of knowing I didn't need to think about anything but me and him. I could breathe.

At least until I told him what I'd discovered.

"Hey! How'd everything go?" I came to greet him at the door. I still may not understand everything he's talking about when it comes to his cars, but I love seeing him light up about his passion.

The rest of the night consisted of listening to the updates, what he thought he needed to do next, snacking, and watching the stupid TV shows that we both loved. Trying to guess what was going to happen and gossiping about the characters we didn't like. The normalcy I needed.

I curled up closer, soaking in his warmth. I was finally letting my mind rest. I knew I wouldn't make it to the room before I fell asleep, but I didn't care. With Wes next to me, I welcomed it, letting it pull me under.

"Aly..." A woman's voice was coming through. Not someone I'd ever heard before. It was faint, but it was there. Everything was so dark. Where was I?

"Aly..." Again, the same faint, soft voice, but I couldn't see where it was coming from or who was speaking.

Then she finally appeared.

"I've been looking for you."

"Who are you?" I had to be dreaming. This couldn't be real. She looked like she was almost glowing with the flowing gray mist that surrounded her.

The last thing I remembered was Wes and I going to sleep.

"My name is Bridget. We've been waiting for you."

Chapter 7

"You've been waiting for me? Who's been waiting for me?" Where even was I? This place was so dark I could still barely see this woman. The fog had spread farther around us, but it was only the two of us standing within it.

"I know this all must be very, very confusing right now." That was an understatement. But her voice was gentle while I was squinting at her, blinking, trying to adjust to the darkness.

"I will explain everything."

"Who are you?"

"My name is Bridget." I think she was just allowing me the moment to ask questions because her name meant nothing to me.

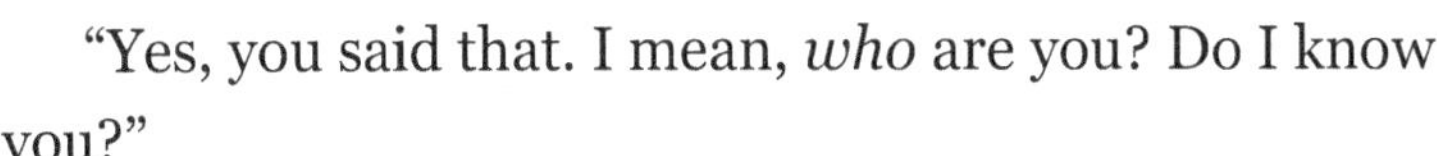

"Yes, you said that. I mean, *who* are you? Do I know you?"

"Not personally, no, but I knew your ancestors."

"The hell does that mean? Is that some kind of riddle?"

"Hush your tone." This time she was a bit more firm. "I understand your frustration, but we do not use that word here."

Here? Her tone made me narrow my eyes, "And where is here exactly?" I gestured to the open space around us covered in fog, "Am I dreaming?" Had this woman brought me here?

"You are and you aren't." She shifted her hands, "It's a bit complicated. You are still physically home, but your mind is here with me. It's more of a dreamlike state, but this place is very real."

"If I'm here, but still home, how much time is going by for me while I'm 'gone'?" What if something happened? I started to worry that I was actually losing time being here.

"Oh, don't worry, time moves at the same pace. Once you leave, you'll wake up and it won't be like you've missed days, weeks, or even years."

"Ok, so will you finally tell me why I'm here and what this place even is?" I wasn't afraid. I was used to having weird dreams. I just wasn't sure how to wake myself out of this one. It seemed I needed to understand the purpose of this place before I could wake up.

"We have been waiting a long time for you, Aly. We need your help. This place, we are actually just outside of it, but I'll take you in. This is what we call The Crypt."

On her word, we were no longer engulfed in darkness but rather standing under a moonlit night sky. I could see now that the two of us were standing in an open field, before a large forest. Her words had cleared the darkness but the fog still remained swirling around us, stretching deep into the trees behind her.

"The Crypt?" I stared in awe at the front line of trees. "This just looks like a creepy forest."

"Well, things are not always what they seem girl." Bridget turned sideways and beckoned me to follow. "Don't worry, you'll be ok with me here."

"Where are we going?"

"I think it'll be easier to explain if you also see for yourself."

Who was this woman? What was I about to walk into? I hesitated, contemplating.

"Time is of the essence. You don't want to oversleep now do you?"

Jesus, it was a tug-of-war in my brain but I was hostage.

Reluctantly, I followed.

Bridget led me through the smallest break in the forest, where somewhat of a path formed that we were able to follow. It was still so dark I couldn't see the actual path in front of me. I had to focus on the trail of Bridget's white dress as she guided me down the beginning of the winding path.

"Do you live in here?" I felt the need to whisper now, the forest was chilling. You felt alone but like you were being watched by God knows what.

"I come and go."

"Well, where are we going if not your home?"

"Patience. You'll see in a moment and I can explain everything."

I could tell I was annoying her slightly but literally, what the hell was going on?

I'm being led through a dark forest, by a strange woman, who says she knew someone in my family? She says I'm basically dreaming, but if this was real, I'd be letting someone lead me to my death...

Or was I dead? Was this a dream state in between? I don't remember what would have happened but am I? I started looking around at everything, as if I'd be able to identify the difference between dream, death, and reality.

Then suddenly, Bridget stopped. I halted behind her. My eyes widened at what was in front of us. We'd stopped just before a large bush, big enough to conceal us both.

"Now quiet. We're fine, but look." Bridget pointed at the large clearing ahead, "Oh, and no, you're not dead or truly dreaming, and I'm not going to kill you. I'm showing you." Did she just read my mind?

I looked towards her pointed hand and passed it, into the clearing, "Who are they? Are they like you? There's so many." People, other people were here? Trapped here? I was trying to count.

"Wandering souls. This is why we call this place The Crypt." Bridget looked back at me, now meeting my eyes, "The Crypt of Lost Souls. This is why we need your help."

I was staring at her blankly, "Me? My help? What can I do?"

"You are able to make the connections with these lost spirits Aly. Why do you think it's been so easy for you? Have you never learned anything about your family history?"

"What does my family's history have to do with this?"

Bridget gave a sigh, "You really never learned any of the truth... I was afraid of that. But it makes sense."

"What makes sense?" Now I was getting a bit more urgent, "What truth am I supposed to know?"

"The other day when you made the first spiritual connection, did it feel easy?" She was calm, more gentle.

"Yes, I wasn't sure why, I thought maybe something was following me or my apartment was haunted." I was shaking now, goosebumps going down my arms.

"And the second time? When you were able to reach two spirits?" She tilted her head and raised a brow at me.

My brows narrowed and I pulled my head back, "Again, my apartment could just be a hotspot for ghosts and spiritual activity. That's all I thought."

Bridget's brow was still raised as she shook her head. I was holding my breath…What did they want from me?

"Aly, I will tell you the story. I will tell you why I am here, why they are here, and what's happening. But you, you fit into all of this because your ancestors are a part of my story. And my story began with the Salem witch trials."

"What are you telling me?" I was frozen. My eyes widening as she continued.

"Allow me to explain Aly, but I'm telling you that you are in fact, a witch."

☙

"A witch?" I just stared in disbelief. This was not happening. "You're telling me that I'm a witch?"

"Yes."

"That's how I was able to connect with those spirits?" Now I was pacing, gesturing with my hands.

"Yes."

Shaking my head, waving my hand, "No, no, that... that's just not possible. You have the wrong person. You have to."

There was no way. How was I a witch and just never knew? I always knew empaths had a greater connection, that's what has helped me. Not because I'm some witch.

"Wait, how did you know about the first time I tried to connect? Have you just been watching me? Like some spiritual spy or something?" Now with a bit of a glaring, accusing tone.

"Not a spy. I was tasked with watching over you... I needed to find a way to hopefully get you here."

"What do you even mean?" I was trying not to yell, I didn't know what kind of attention that would attract. "If all of this is supposedly true, why have I never known? Why are you only here now?" Was my whole life a lie? This couldn't actually be possible...

"I was not allowed to make the connection first. There was a curse, I was mostly spared, but that was one rule I had to follow."

"Oh, of course. Now there's a curse too." I threw my hands and just looked at the clearing.

"I will explain from the beginning if you'll allow me." Bridget's shoulders had dropped. She was defeated. I didn't really care in this moment though. I was fuming, but also, nothing made sense. I felt like so many things could be a lie.

"Why should I believe anything anymore?" Now I was a bit defeated.

"That's valid. But considering where we are and what you can see, would you at least like to know before making that decision?"

I stopped pacing and just looked at her, "Fine. Fair. Explain."

Normally, I probably would've found a log or stump close by as a seat to listen, but not now. It wasn't as dark as what Bridget had first created, but it hadn't exactly lit up with sunlight. The fog was still rolling around us and I was not fully certain things weren't lurking within.

Instead I stood, crossing my arms, waiting for her to begin this story that, in her words, explained everything.

"I assume you've at least known about the Salem trials?" I nodded. "Ok good. That's where this all starts."

I simply waited for her to begin.

"Back when this all started, it was during the Salem witch trials. Our coven was there, in Salem and nearby. That's also how I knew your ancestors. They were members of the coven. We were a family.

"But the villagers speculations began to happen. Obviously, we were all nervous, but we didn't think it would end so badly. We thought we could lay low for a while and it would all be ok. We were very careful.

"Back then, you couldn't even risk the accusation. The trials weren't really trials. They were tests." She paused to look at me. I nodded, acknowledging that I was following. Everyone who had learned about the witch trials at least knew this much. So she continued...

"One day, I had an altercation with another member, another witch in the coven. She was a baker and she was upset with another villager. She didn't want to hurt anyone, she just wanted to mess with them a little bit.

"She came to me because I provided holistic remedies to the village. She wanted me on her side, especially if anything went a little sideways. But I got mad. I told her no. Not that I wouldn't be on her side if she was accused, but that what she wanted to do was just too risky.

"She wasn't happy with that. She couldn't stand not getting her way."

Bridget seemed to be bringing herself back to that time in her life. She began pacing, her hands getting more expressive with each step.

"I was so worried by her pride, anger, and pettiness in that moment. I understood why she was frustrated. Who we were was being throttled because of the villagers and this new fear. But we didn't want to leave our home.

"We were also torn by the fact of, if we did leave, if we did want to. Would that be too obvious? All of us leaving at once. Would people look at us as being afraid of being accused so accuse us anyway? The trials might just continue anyway before we could escape or if we could escape would they still come after us?

"So I understood, but I knew we still needed to wait. So I did the only thing I thought would stop her. I was the coven leader's second, her right hand. I told her that if she continued with her plan I would have no choice but to report her to the leader, Madam Selene. Of course, the villagers knew her only as Selene.

"Our argument ended there and she stormed out of my shop. Honestly, I didn't know what she planned to do in that moment so I was nervous. She stormed out and hadn't given her word otherwise, so I went to Madam Selene right away.

"A whole longer story short. She found out I went to the leader and changed her plans. In her anger and vengeful state, instead of going after the annoying villager, she went after me.

"She brought accusations and skepticism to the town leaders because of my shop—because of how I was helping people. It wasn't necessarily wrong, but she turned on me. She turned on the coven."

Bridget stopped pacing. She actually looked saddened, re-living the last moments of her past friendship. The past, learning that one of her own had been so angry that they chose to betray her in the worst way.

Bridget had, in a way, betrayed her own sister, but for safety, not hatred.

"I was so afraid. I didn't know what to do. Back then we were able to connect to each other mentally. When you shared the coven bond, you could do that. I was hiding in my shop and all I could do was call out to Madam Selene through that bond.

"Thankfully, she was right there. She came through and simply told me she was sorry, everything was going to be ok, and she would handle it. But, she told me that if things went south, I would end up in a safe place, waiting for our return.

"Of course, I didn't fully understand it at the time, but she said it would be our return. She would make it so. All I could do was trust her. And once she said that, the village soldiers burst through my shop door to take me away."

She paused again to look at me, awaiting any questions I may have yet.

"Ok, that's a lot so far. But how does my family fit in? What exactly happened? What was her plan? Because obviously you're here."

"Yes. Well, obviously, things went south. I was put on trial and I failed. No one ever passed. We aren't immortal and of course they'll just kill you anyway if you do anything to actually escape. I had to let them win. I was the first witch killed during the trials.

"But Madam Selene came through on what she said. I ended up here. It's not necessarily a good place now, but it wasn't always terrible. It was just a waiting room.

"And Selene also showed up. She came to me again to tell me she was sorry and that I had done the right thing. She told me that she had cursed the coven as punishment. She didn't want that to happen again. So if another witch was the reason you went to trial, the accusing witch was sent here and became eternally stuck, wandering forever. If you were a witch who simply died, you were sent here to wait.

"I asked her what exactly we were waiting for and she told me, the descendants born with the ancestors power. I would know because they would be named after or in honor of the witches we knew. I couldn't look for you, I couldn't tell you what you were and I couldn't try to convince you. I had to wait for the descendant to find their own connection and then I could step in. Only then and that was also my job.

"And you're here now. I heard your call as soon as you made that first connection. It was like everything connected. I haven't even heard Madam Selene's voice since I came here. But that day even her voice came through the bond saying you and your sister's names, Aly. I knew you had finally made your connection and now I could make mine."

Bridget took a breath and looked back at me. She had been staring through the fog at the forest floor for a long time through this last part.

"I knew I could finally bring you here, tell you everything, and show you how we needed your help. Now more than ever."

"Now more than ever?" I questioned, "What could have gotten worse?" She'd just been waiting and basically wandering, sounded pretty awful already.

"Well, see, it's not just witches coming here anymore. Someone else has taken over, and now any and all lost souls end up here. People who died but haven't crossed over and even people who haven't died but their minds are wandering in the in-between trying to find their way back. Pretty much—on accident, we've created a limbo."

I took a breath. This was so much to process. I was just trying to have some fun with my sister and now I've gotten myself in the middle of some kind of witch vs ghost warfare? I wasn't trying to fight ghosts. I wasn't claiming to be a witch! Dammit, Maia, I was just trying to play with some crystals, dammit!

Trying to collect myself, I looked back at Bridget, "To be honest, I don't really know what to say...but what exactly am I supposed to do about this limbo? I'm trying to process but this is a lot. You say I'm a witch but I haven't exactly been practicing my entire life..."

"This place has been taken over. You connected with that dark energy remember?"

I nodded, how could I forget.

"That wasn't just a dark energy. And that first nicer spirit wasn't a witch." My eyes narrowed, "That first spirit was a wanderer from here. They aren't dead yet, but they need help getting back to their body. That dark energy… That wasn't just another spirit," Her voice lowered, "That was him. The Reaper."

I stared, blinking at her, "The Reaper. As in Grim, The Grim Reaper?"

"Yes."

"Am I supposed to be fighting The Grim Reaper?" I made an incredulous face. She had to be joking now.

"You are a connector. We need to help the wanderers find their way back to their bodies. Save them. Then, yes, I need your help, to kill The Reaper and destroy this place."

Chapter 8

Jolting awake, I jerked forward, gasping for air. It felt like I'd woken up straight out of a panic attack with the tightness in my chest.

Catching my breath, I frantically scanned my surroundings. I was alone, but I was back in my living room. At least there was that. Putting a hand to my chest, working on long slow breaths to calm myself back down, I slumped back down into the couch.

I was home. I was ok. I wasn't dead. At least, not yet. But what was that?

Wait... Where was Wes? I was alone. When I'd fallen asleep he was next to me. Did he just go to bed? All the lights, other than the dim corner lamp, were off. Lunging forward again, I snatched my phone off the ottoman to check the time.

10 AM! It was the next day! I mean, I hadn't lost that much time, but still!

So where was Wes?

Finally I noticed the note that had been next to my phone.

"Went to my parents to work on the car more. I didn't want to wake you. Love you, I'll see you later."

Ok, I let out a breath. Everything was ok. My whole body relaxed, dropping back down against the couch. I hated dreams like that—they felt way too real, too jarring. It never failed to take me a minute or two to recollect myself.

This one felt even more different though... Way more real than normal. I've had vivid dreams that I knew were dreams, when I was in the middle of them. This one hadn't felt the same... But I couldn't have really been there... I was home now. I've been home. I was dreaming. I literally just woke up. Was I losing it? Legitimately, was this the beginning of actually losing my mind?

In my normal dreams, even when they felt the most real, I still just move through them. I talk to people, I understand what's going on or know that whatever's happening shouldn't be. I'm now realizing, the one thing that never happens, is my senses have never truly been involved. I can see and hear my surroundings but I can't smell or feel what I'm touching... I can't feel the warmth or the cold, I can't smell the air around me. I'll know I'm sitting on a chair but I won't feel the chair. I can walk but I'm not feeling the ground. This time, it was everything.

How could that even be possible? Some ghost, witch lady just invaded my dream? Or maybe got into my subconscious? But why could I feel the brush and the dirt under my feet? How I could smell the grass, the leaves, and the must of the forest surrounding us?

No, no. That couldn't be possible... Could it?

I grabbed my phone to message Maia, "I just had the strangest dream."

"Huh..." Was all she said. She had responded quickly enough to my message that I just decided to call.

"That's it? Huh?" What did she mean huh?

"Well, it is strange... That's really interesting. But do you think with everything else going on that it really was just a weird dream?"

Maia's tone sounded strange. I narrowed my eyes and kind of side-eyed the phone. Wes wasn't home so I had her on speaker.

"What do you mean? What else do you think it was? That couldn't have been real."

"No, I'm not saying you were really there in the woods, but, I don't know, maybe it was like a vision or something."

"A vision?" My voice raised slightly, now visions… No, no, that definitely wasn't it… What am I, *That's So Raven* now?

"Or something! I'm just throwing out ideas. It is weird that the connections are coming so easily. Now this?"

"So what? Do you think we're witches now?"

"No, I didn't say that, it's just weird. I mean ok, with everything else we know, where do we even go from here?"

I took a breath. I needed to relax. It wasn't a vision. I wasn't in the woods, it was just a crazy dream. But maybe there was some slight truth to it.

"Dreams are normally created from situations and events currently happening in our lives, plus any added stress. Maybe I painted a really elaborate picture last night, but maybe there are still some spirits that need help. We did connect with at least one the other day."

"That would make sense." I could hear the agreeing shrug in Maia's tone.

"But wait, who are we helping?

"That I don't know, I guess we'd have to find out." I made my way to the kitchen and was fidgeting with a pen on the counter.

After a moment's pause, Maia responded, "And, ok, I'm not saying we are…" She was tip-toeing, nervous to even suggest what she was about to, "But if the dream wasn't just a dream... If everything were true... Would that be so bad?"

Was that what she wanted? She wanted this to be real? I didn't even know what to say.

"Maia, everything about that place felt terrible. It didn't feel fun or exciting. It didn't feel like going on an adventure, like when we went to that one haunted hotel. It was cold, and chilling, and seeing those people just wandering around was sad.... I... I don't know."

"And I get that. I'm not saying it's a place to go back to. I'm saying, if it was real, those people actually do need help."

How was she a voice of reason in this situation right now?

"Well, if it was real, why hasn't anyone come to you yet?" I had to challenge. I could just believe any of this yet.

She paused on the other end. "Maia?"

"I don't know," was all she said.

"I need a shower." I needed a break, from thinking, from this conversation, from everything. Just a real, honest break and a hot shower sounded amazing right now. "That dream didn't help my sleep so I need to wake up a bit. I'll text you in a bit."

I stood there, letting the water rush over me, the heat warming my skin, the steam rising around me. How did I always forget how good this felt? How something so simple can be so peaceful. I should've thought of some aromatherapy or bath salts just as an extra touch. Next time.

I didn't care how long I was standing there. I'm pretty sure this was my first real chance at alone time in the last week and a half, ever since all of this started. All my time had been spent either working, focusing on me and Wes, or if I did have 'alone time' I was preparing for or doing this investigating with Maia. I hadn't taken a real moment to take care of myself.

But now, in the heat of the shower, I would stand here until the water ran cold. I had some time to think.

I had been denying that dream all morning.

Bridget, she told me her name was Bridget. She was the first witch killed during the trials… And Maia and I were both named after or in honor of other witches… It sounded insane. Some things made sense though. If it was a dream, it would still make sense for her to know about the connections I had made. What still didn't make sense is why I had been able to feel and smell everything.

Then I got an idea. I think I knew what I needed to do next if I was going to figure this out for sure. As much as I'd love to live in the denial, I had to know. If there were spirits that needed help, what would happen if I just rejected it? I knew what I had to do.

I wasn't jumping into any seance to summon Bridget right away, but I needed to know if what Bridget had said was true. I had to confirm.

With the water going cold, as if my decision had caused it, I shut off the shower and grabbed the towel. Today I was definitely staying home so comfy clothes it was—a hoodie and leggings, it was like my safety blanket.

Taking a seat at the office desk, I took a breath. Here goes nothing.

Salem Witch Trials, I typed into the search bar. If Bridget was the first one on trial there had to be some record of that. There should be recordings for all of them. Come to think of it, it kind of seemed strange that we never did learn any names from those trials or even a number for how many trials were held.

A list of articles populated the search—going down the history, why the trials happened, what started the speculations, and what people did to accuse. There were even websites about a museum dedicated to the trials, but still nothing with a list of names.

There had to be a list.

I adjusted my search, *Names of witches killed in the Salem witch trials*, and hit enter. Just like that, the top article.

My hand sat hovering over the mouse. I couldn't bring myself to click the link right away. I didn't know who was on that list, so if what Bridget said was true, what would that mean? Was the rest of it real too?

No, her name could be there, she may or may not be first, but there was still more to know. It's fine. I just had to hit the damn button.

I took a breath and clicked to open the link. The list sat just below where the webpage started, but there it was. Bridget's name. The first one on the list for accused and executed... I couldn't even say what I was expecting. I don't know. I was frozen. Part of me was expecting this, part of me had a strange feeling that I knew it would be true. But I had hoped, I hoped I was wrong. I hoped I was going crazy at this point and there was no way it could actually be true.

I had never looked this up before. I never would have had that bit of information in my brain to even create a nightmare that felt so real. How was this possible? I felt like I was silently screaming in my head now.

But that's just one thing. Maybe the others wouldn't add up. Then it would just be weird. I could deal with weird. Weird was better than it being real.

She'd said we were named after the other witches... So I kept scrolling.

There were a few names to start, nothing for Maia yet. But I realized, 'Maia' probably would not be a name used back in that period. Bridget had also said in honor of... Could Maia be a nickname? I didn't want this to be real, but I couldn't just pretend anymore, I had to be sure. It didn't help anything to just keep denying unless I was denying a false reality.

I pulled up a new tab for a new search. *What can Maia be a shortened version of?* Not many. But Martha. Martha was on this list, and the witch trials list. Maia was named for Martha...

My hands started shaking again. It didn't take much more scrolling to see another witch on that list. My name didn't even need a search. I knew as soon as I saw it. Alice. My full name was Alison. That didn't take guesswork or a genius...

Bridget was the first witch and we were named after Martha and Alice. How did we never know about this? How was this kept secret for so long? Why would it *be* a secret?

I was still shaking but not the same anymore. I was shocked, confused, angry, I still had no idea what this all truly meant, but even more now, I couldn't keep pretending. I couldn't keep denying. I wasn't one hundred percent on us possessing any sort of power or being witches, that seemed a little too much, even with all of this. But that dream was more than just a dream and Bridget was telling the truth.

I needed to call Maia.

"You confirmed it?" Maia was in shock, disbelief, maybe even a little excited.

"Bridget was at least telling the truth about who she was and who we are." I had bundled up on my couch with a heated blanket. I needed the comfort. "You were right. I don't know what that was, but it definitely was not just a dream."

"This is insanity!" It sounded like she was pacing.

"Are you happy? Are you ok? Freaked out?" I really wasn't sure about this reaction. I didn't even know how to feel yet.

"Well, I mean it is a little freaky, but kind of in an exciting way, no?"

"Uhh..." I'd lost all sense on how to respond to her at this point.

"I mean, you have to talk to her again now."

"Are you just having fun using me as some kind of spiritual guinea pig?" I narrowed my eyes at the phone. It's times like these that I wished Maia lived closer. Then she could at least experience my expressions and gestures in person when she talked like this.

"Well she didn't come to ME first, now did she?"

"I can't just summon her, I'm pretty sure she summoned me first." I was back to fidgeting with my pen. I'll call it my comfort pen, I kind of wanted to flick it across the room.

"Wait, why do I need to talk to her again?" Maia was oddly encouraging about this part.

"She said there were spirits that needed help didn't she?"

"She did, but wouldn't we just try to connect with them then?" I knew she was probably right. I just didn't want to go back to that creepy, musty, forest.

"We could, but you already confirmed what she said…"

"I don't want to go back to that forest Maia." I finally just said it. I didn't. If it was possible not to, I didn't want to.

"Based off what she said, we may eventually have to be back there. But I get it."

I had to think for a moment.

"If we try to connect again, what happened last time may just happen again. If you take the moment to try to just reach out to Bridget again, we could get the answers we need. From what you said, it seemed like she was trying to guide you. She's not trying to trap you there." Maia had heard my sigh, heard me take a minute. She knew I was trying to think when she'd finally spoken. "I think this is the better way."

"I just don't understand why it's only been me so far too. Like, you've been going through all of this with me. Why has she only contacted me?"

"I...I don't know. Maybe she needs your help the most." Why was Maia so calm about all of this?

"You do know how insane all of this sounds, right?" I really couldn't get over it. Maia was so quick to accept. "I don't know how you're staying so calm." Oh wait, maybe because she wasn't the one going back into a creepy, dark, foggy forest to talk to a ghost witch from our ancestors past!

My head was spinning.

"I just choose to be. It's a lot, but if it's all true, it is kind of exciting... You can't completely deny that."

"I thought being a witch would be more fun." I was pouting. That's all I could do in protest now. "Alright, fine. I'm going to get setup and I'll call you back." Tossing out some additional choice words while I could before hanging up the phone.

Candles, stones, and I guess make this space as peaceful as possible. Let's see if I could even get my brain to meditate.

"Are you calm?" Maia was on speaker. I was sitting on the ground, crisscross, eyes closed. I was trying to relax... Now raising a brow, giving Maia a face through the phone without even opening my eyes.

"I feel like you're giving me a look..."

"Maia, you're not helping."

"Ok, ok, you're still there, sorry. I'll be quiet." I could feel her hands going up in defense at the phone. "I'm here if you need me."

I slowed and steadied my breathing. The last time it had been a dream. I didn't know how to go back to that place on my own. There had been something else Bridget had said, what was it? I hadn't thought about it until now...

The bond! I could try calling down the bond. Could I even access it? I mean if my ancestors were within the coven it was possible? It didn't hurt to try.

I wasn't sure exactly how it worked, so I started in my head first. *Bridget? Are you there?*

My arms started to tingle and my chest warmed... *Bridget? Is that you trying to reach me?*

Maybe I needed a stronger push. This time I spoke it out loud, "Bridget? If the bond is there, I'm trying to bring you in."

Maia gasped, realizing what I was doing. "Say you're throwing a tether! A tether through the bond!" She whispered, but it was practically a scream whisper.

I repeated her words, "Bridget, I'm throwing a tether, a tether through the bond. Can you come to me?"

The warmth in my chest grew, my arms, hands, and fingers were all tingling now. I felt a rush come over me and then her voice. My eyes were still closed.

"You've accepted the bond." I opened my eyes. Bridget was standing by the door.

She looked the same as she had in the woods and now she was smiling.

My heart began racing, my palms suddenly wet, she was here. It worked. I didn't have to go to the creepy, foggy forest yet. I put a hand to the warmth that was still in my chest.

"Don't worry, you get used to it." Bridget acknowledged, understanding more than I did apparently.

"Is she there? Did it work?" Maia was anxiously waiting.

"Uh-yea," I was still staring in shock, "It worked."

"Thank you for your help Maia." Bridget hadn't spoken the words, but I heard them in my head. She was speaking to both of us.

"Maia? Thank you? What is she talking about Maia?" What was going on?

"I also visited Maia. You have nothing to worry about." Bridget began to explain, "I knew you were skeptical. You were still in shock when you left the woods. I asked Maia to help get you to give me another shot."

I was shocked, baffled, also enraged. So many emotions feeling ready to explode when we were trying to figure out more. I thought we were trying to learn and figure this out together.

"You knew?" I stared directly at the phone.

"Don't be mad, let me explain." Maia was already defensive.

But I stopped her, "This whole time I was freaking out, about the dream, trying to confirm things. I was so unsure about what Bridget had said. But you knew. And she came to you too."

Chapter 9

"I didn't know everything! Just hold on. Let me explain." Maia was firm but calm. I glared at the phone, I could tell she was trying to avoid me hanging up right then and there.

"She knew just as much as you, Aly." This time coming from Bridget. It felt like an ambush.

Whether Maia knew more than me or not didn't matter. She'd still kept this from me. "Why didn't you tell me, Maia? I was telling you how confused I was. That I didn't understand why I would be the only one being directly affected. Why wouldn't you tell me she also came to you?"

"You needed to choose to believe this for yourself." Bridget interjected before Maia could even try to answer, "It's my fault. My request to Maia. The bond doesn't work as well if you're holding any doubt. It can't be forced."

"And Maia was different?"

"I don't know what it was Aly, but when Bridget came to me I just felt... Connected in a way I couldn't explain."

"The difference was," Bridget cut back in, "Maia wanted to believe. With everything happening, I could tell she wanted an explanation. The difference was... In her glow."

"Her glow?" Now I raised a brow. Also slightly offended. "You're telling me my aura was off?"

"No, no, not necessarily... More like, she was ready for the information. You had a more protective spark around you."

"Huh..." I tapped my finger to my chin, "I mean, maybe that's because I was learning about everything in a dark, creepy forest with someone I'd never met and dead people were walking around everywhere." I gave her a look as if to add, "Interesting." At the end.

"Fair."

"I still didn't know everything for sure." I wondered if Maia was getting annoyed with Bridget explaining her side for her. "She just told me what she told you. I knew you still needed to see it for yourself to really believe. I was only asked to help get you back for another conversation."

"By tricking me." I was still angry.

"I'm sorry! Ok. Like you said, ghost lady. What was I supposed to do?... Sorry Bridget, no offense."

"None taken."

"How did you know it wasn't dangerous?"

"Do you really think I would do that? You're the one who's been contacting some dark energy this whole time." Maia sighed, "After most of our conversation I figured this was at least safer than that."

The dark energy... I'd almost forgotten... The part I had actually left out of telling Maia about...

I sighed, looking at Bridget, she returned a knowing look and nodded. She hadn't said anything either. If I got too mad now how upset would Maia be later when she learned what I had kept from her? Even though there was still uncertainty in the future of that, it was something I wasn't ready to bring up.

"Ok... Ok... I get it. This is just a lot, all of it. But we're here now, so let's just move on... Deal?"

"Deal, I'm sorry, no more."

I looked at Bridget and she raised a brow, looking directly into my eyes.

"Maia can't hear either of us right now, I closed her out for this, just think your response to me." My eyes stayed trained on her, waiting. "You don't want her to know about The Reaper yet, correct?"

I shook my head, "One thing at a time and not until it's necessary." If this couldn't be all fun and games for me, I could at least keep it feeling like a fun adventure for Maia.

"We may need her help eventually." Bridget acknowledged, pressing me to do the same.

"Then we'll deal with that later."

Bridget nodded and released my gaze.

"Hello? Still there? God I hate being stuck on this phone sometimes." We'd gone silent, "I said I was sorry!"

"Yes, yes, sorry, still here. Bridget is going to connect with us so we can start figuring things out."

"Ok ladies," She'd locked back into our minds, "Ask away. What do you want to know? We have spirits to help."

Bridget wasn't just speaking aloud anymore. Now there was an even stranger sensation. It was like a creeping knock on my inner thoughts. She wasn't just trying to dive deeper into our minds—she was connecting with her own. And we had to let her in.

I let my eyes close and my head lean back, giving in and accepting the connection.

"You have accepted the coven bond. We are all connected now. But more than that, we are family now." I could hear the smile in Bridget's voice.

This new place started out dark but as Bridget spoke it was like our minds were connecting into a whole separate reality. It felt like another dimension. Standing together, we formed a triangle, Maia to my right, Bridget to my left. The only light was coming from us in the middle of our formation—only to see each other. Like a little hiding place in our minds. I looked at Maia who met my gaze and started smiling.

Just when I think things can't get any weirder… My luck one ups me. Classic.

"Can we call on you at any time?" Maia asked.

"You can call, you can reach out, however, I may not always be able to come in the same form as I have today. But you'll always hear me. If something is happening, I will help how I can."

So we wouldn't be completely alone.

"Who are the wandering souls?" My turn for a question.

"Mm…" Bridget took a moment and closed her eyes, "Those poor souls."

I exchanged glances with Maia. How long had this been happening? How long had she been helplessly watching? Was something else happening?

"Yes, those poor souls are the ones trapped. They are the souls of injured people who are waiting to be found again so they can fully heal. But unfortunately, those souls don't know where they are."

"Do they know they're not dead yet?" Maia asked. I could tell she already felt sad for these souls.

"I don't know for sure, but considering where they end up, until it completely happens, I think they already think so."

"Until what completely happens?" She hadn't mentioned this to me yet.

"They're wandering. They look lost until a certain day comes... You can tell when they lose their...tether to the world." Bridget seemed unsure how to answer. Did The Reaper have something to do with this? Was she trying not to say too much in front of Maia?

"So, their human body is their tether... You're saying if the person dies, in the human world, the human reality, the soul is trapped where it is?" We weren't giving them a bridge to cross, we were throwing them a rope...

"Essentially, yes." Bridget confirmed. "And that is not the place you want to be when you die." She looked right at me as she said it. Clearly, she wasn't saying more with Maia present, this was her signal. It did have to do with The Reaper.

What was happening to these people if they got trapped?

"Have you seen anyone make it back to their body?" A valid question from Maia. If everyone got stuck, eventually how do you tell who's still wandering and lost?

How many would be in the place Bridget called The Crypt at this point?

"Fortunately, I have known some to find their way home. But it seems those tethers were either not as damaged or it was much more of a temporary absence to be separated. If they find their way back, they were not gone long." Bridget explained.

"So how do we help?" Maia seemed done with questions, ready for a plan. "If they need to find their tether, their human body again, how do we do that?"

"Well, that will be the trickier part." Bridget admitted. "They don't know what happened, or where they are... But they still remember their names and who they are."

"Almost like a trauma response." I realized, "Maybe if their spirit is thinking they are trying to find peace, that also means blocking out the event."

"That could very well be it." Bridget looked like she hadn't even thought of that. Which made sense. She had been concerned seeing these spirits just come and go for God knows how long now.

"So what does that mean?" Maia looked at me.

"It means we don't need to figure out what happened to them. People get transferred from hospitals all the time. Even if we knew what and where, that may mean nothing."

"Ok? So, it means we have nothing?"

"No, we just need to learn about them. Their name and where they were. Maybe even a most recent memory, but we'll have to do some researching ourselves."

"Ok, but the other question... How are we supposed to help them?" Maia turned to Bridget, "You've seen this for years and haven't been able to help..."

Bridget sighed, not in frustration, but in sadness, disappointment in her own situation.

"I'm not connected with the human world the same way as I once was. I'm not able to act in the same capacity as you two. But, from what I've witnessed so far, I believe you both are connectors. One of your many abilities."

Abilities. Plural.

"Connectors?" This time I was questioning. Did that mean something other than us just being able to connect with this other side?

"Yes, connectors." Bridget nodded, "I believe you are able to bridge the gap."

I must have given her a confused look because she simply continued.

"In essence, if you find the person the spirit is connected to, you can act as the bridge that brings them back together. You can *reconnect* them." She added a bit of emphasis on the simple word she seemed to like so much now.

"So, we would be like a guiding light back to their body." Maia's eyes had widened and brightened as she looked from me to Bridget. "Aly, we could literally be saving people from slipping away! Going towards the wrong light... Or well, the light when it's not really their time yet!"

Maia just really wanted to help people. I understood.

"Precisely." Bridget smiled now, having Maia at least very on board.

"There's only one problem, I'm not sure it's really a problem, but something to think about." I needed things fleshed out. There could be problems and it was better to address now. "If we are with the person, we'll need to be able to get out before they fully come to. Since no one has been doing this, we don't know if they would remember us or know what happened. We don't want to risk that."

"Agreed." Bridget was on my side. Good. Made sense after what she's gone through. "That is something we need to think about."

"But if we're on the same page there..." I hesitated, I knew I couldn't say no, but I really didn't want to say yes. I closed my eyes and gave a quiet sigh, "I'm in."

Maia was giddy. "Me too!" Clapping her hands, a huge smile breaking across her face.

Almost instantly, Maia and Bridget disappeared and I felt the jerk back to reality. A little harsh, but maybe this was something I'd have to get used to? Opening my eyes, I was back in the office. Bridget was still here.

I let out a breath I didn't realize I'd even been holding.

"Wait, what just happened?" Maia's voice called back through the phone speaker, "Did something go wrong?"

I looked to Bridget for her response. I had no idea, everything had ended so suddenly.

"No, nothing went wrong. This is simply the easiest way for me to communicate with you both." Bridget reassured, "I don't have as much strength as I once did." She still wasn't speaking aloud, only echoed in our minds.

Her comment made me realize, it wasn't just the easiest way, it was the only way to speak with both of us at the same time without Maia present. It made sense... She was still technically the spirit of a witch after all—they weren't really known for being able to chat over the phone.

So within the bond it would have to stay.

"Oh, ok, I see." Maia was relieved, though slightly concerned. "But are you ok? Do you need to rest?"

"Oh Maia, you're very kind but I'm ok now. This isn't nearly as straining."

"So... As long as you're ok... *How* do we start?" I was just trying to get us back on track.

"Yes, yes. Back to that." Bridget adjusted herself against the wall, trying to get comfortable. Watching her, I couldn't help but wonder, could she actually feel the wall? Could she feel it or just not pass through it?

"Would you like to sit down?" I gestured to the spot on the floor across from me.

She paused, a brief moment of hesitation. She had the look of someone who hadn't known a moment's rest for a very long time.

"Can I feel you while you're here? You could sit and we join hands if that could help our connection." I actually hadn't even thought of it until this moment.

It seemed Bridget hadn't either, but her eyes brightened, "Oh, yes, we could give it a shot."

She took her place in front of me on the floor and put out her hands, "You'll have to forgive me. I've waited so long for the two of you and I've had no one to really practice with... Sometimes I forget the things that could be possible."

This comment finally won her a smile from me as I took her hands. "At least that makes two of us with not knowing what's possible."

"This is so damn unfair!" Maia's voice came yelling out the speaker, "I can hear you on the phone and in my head — but all I want is to just crawl through this phone and be there."

"Oh hush, Maia. We'll be fighting demons soon enough and you'll regret ever wanting that." I rolled my eyes at the phone as if she was really there. Honestly, this new bond actually made it feel like Maia was really there. It was like I could mentally feel her hand on my shoulder. It was kind of nice, even when she was annoying.

Maia huffed, but I gestured to Bridget to continue.

"As I was saying… Maia, can you still hear me?" Bridget spoke nothing aloud, but it came through loud and clear.

"Mhmm…" Maia, still slightly annoyed, "I think it's actually a little better, you don't sound as distant."

"Amazing…" Bridget looked like she could feel it too. She looked at me, wondering.

I looked at my hands slightly confused, I wasn't sure how to put it in the right words.

"It doesn't quite feel like the touch of a hand, but I can still feel something there… And then I just feel power. It… It's almost like a surge."

It was working, but nowhere near what I imagined.

"Oh. my. God." It sounded like Maia threw something.

"Don't worry, Maia. You'll get to feel it too." Bridget smiled and went to continue. "Ok, back to the matter at hand. Now I know you have concerns, Aly, and we can address those. We can make sure we have our bases covered. But first, we need to discuss getting the first spirit connected to you. We're all aware that the last time it worked it wasn't exactly in good company. This time can be different. It will be planned."

"Earlier, you said there were many wandering souls… How many are we helping this first time?" I felt this was a valid question. Maybe I was jumping ahead a little bit, but it wasn't like things were slowing down. Everything only seemed to move faster the more we learned.

"For now, to make sure everything goes well, we'll start with one. Start testing your ability. I have someone in mind that's been wandering for quite some time." She paused a moment. Watching these souls every day, not knowing when their unfortunate last day would come truly affected her, you could tell. "I don't know how long they have left…" Her stare moved to the ground, "So if this can work, I feel it's important to start getting the most imperative out first."

I was nodding, that all made sense so far.

"You said, for now. Does that mean we could do more?" Maia came through now. I swear every question she asked sounded excited.

"It does. It's possible. But that's why we need to trial first. We need to see the possibilities."

"If we're able to and need to help so many, how would we do that? We couldn't possibly go to every place these people are to guide their spirits back." I understood helping the spirits, but I couldn't just hop on a plane to go find multiple patients, multiple hospitals, or who knows where they were, who's souls were trying to find their way back. No matter how much I wanted to help…

"Not physically, no."

I raised a brow. "Not physically?"

It sounded like Maia dropped something. I don't think she was expecting that answer either.

"This is why the first test is important." Bridget nodded and continued. "We need to make sure you can bridge. Then we can make sure you can guide."

"So we're essentially training to become spirit tour guides?" I just sat there, blinking at her. I said things just kept getting weirder and weirder... first seeing ghosts, then I have Salem ancestors, then I'm a witch with a calling, connecting with my sister and a ghost witch completely with our minds—no need for verbal communication, although Maia and I still chose to interject it at times, now I can mentally transport spirits back to their bodies before they're dead?... Seriously, what would be next? Oh yea, fighting The Reaper... Right.

Bridget gave a slight laugh to my comment, "Destination — home body."

I took a deep breath, "So how do we avoid, one, being seen by the person if we can reconnect them, and two, Mr. Negative for this first one?"

"Well, that first one should be a little more simple. We can look into some cloaking spells, but I think the safest bet is removing yourself as soon as the connection is made. Not waiting for the person to wake up." She gave a little shrug, "We also don't know if they will wake up right away... We aren't miracle workers. Our job is just making sure they're reconnected so they can complete their healing."

"And we'll know when that happens?"

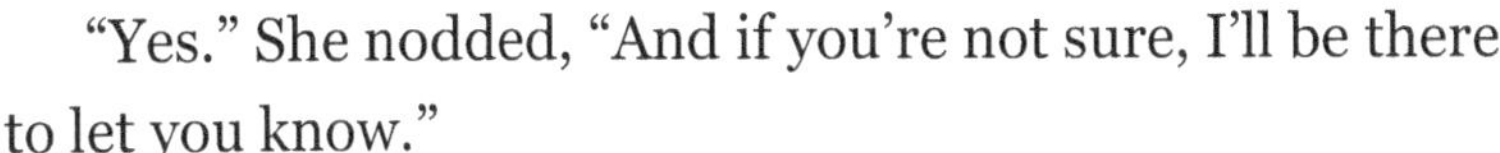

"Yes." She nodded, "And if you're not sure, I'll be there to let you know."

"As for Mr. Negative?"

Though she had slight hesitation, Bridget gave a smirk to my nickname, "As for him... How do you feel about coming to the forest again?"

My stomach dropped, was that the only option?

"In another dream?" Maybe I could deal with that...

Bridget looked sympathetically at me, my hands had begun to shake and she could feel the tremble. But she nodded.

"Can Maia join me this time? Can you connect us both?"

"I can definitely try."

"Tonight?" Maia actually sounded into it. I did feel bad. She didn't know what to really expect, but, at least I would be there. And we'd be avoiding The Reaper.

Bridget smiled at the urgency and looked at me for confirmation. I took a breath and ultimately nodded.

"Tonight it is." Bridget nodded. "Thank you both very much."

Bridget dropped my hands and simultaneously I felt her slip from my mind. It was like she was a thread weaving the three of us together and it became untied.

"Ok, Maia. I think that's it... We've got a plan and I need to get things cleaned up here." I spoke the words though I was still so unsure of what we were about to do.

"Eek! Ok! See you in our dreams! Oh this is crazy." Click, she hung up. I couldn't help but laugh at her excitement.

I looked back at Bridget, "I know you left things out. She doesn't know what happens after we help these people, but what is happening to them now? What is happening once their tether is gone and they get stuck?"

We were both still on the floor. Again, she looked defeated, as if there was something she'd been trying to stop.

"I haven't been able to do anything myself and I haven't been able to connect with anyone for help."

"Bridget. What's happening?" I pressed. I didn't want excuses. I didn't blame her for anything. I just needed to know.

"The Reaper." She practically blurted it, "The Reaper is happening."

Her tone dropped and she met my wide-eyed gaze, "He's waiting for these poor souls to lose their tether so he can take them away."

"Take them where?" My brows narrowed.

"That, I don't know. I assume a worse place. His leader? I just know they don't come back."

"His leader? He's not the leader?" From what she'd told me already, what could be worse than that place?

"No, he can't be. The leader is never the one to fetch. He has to be working for someone."

So we weren't just saving people from that place. The never-ending wandering of the Crypt. We weren't just saving them from The Reaper, who I thought was just keeping them there... It was so much worse.

"So we're not just racing time... We're racing against The Reaper..."

Chapter 10

I knew she had to leave but I had to ask one more thing. "Before we do this, before we take Maia into that place, just tell me, do we have a chance of running into him?" I couldn't stress this question enough.

Bridget understood, "He doesn't come for the living. He arrives only when someone loses their tether. But, he does have an entry point and I've become very sensitive to his presence. I've also become very sensitive to knowing when someone becomes stuck." She took my hand and looked into my eyes, "It's not one hundred percent, but if I get any sense that he's there or if we see him, I will get you both out right away."

I felt tears burning behind my eyes at her words. I hadn't even realized just how much I'd been holding back —how frightening and real this was all becoming.

"You two are helping me more than you know." She could sense my worry. I wasn't sure if it was painted on my face, because of the bond or both. "I will protect you the best I possibly can… I'd say with my life, but, well…" She put her hands up in a small joking shrug.

That did make me laugh.

"Thank you for trusting me." She was being genuine. She couldn't do this without us and she truly wanted to save these people.

"I'll see you in my dreams." I gave her a gentle smile, letting her know she could be excused. I think she needed to feel ok to leave, feel like she wasn't just vanishing.

Bridget smiled back and I watched her fade into nothing. As if no one was ever here.

I was alone. Bridget was gone, Maia wasn't on the phone, but why did it feel a little strange now? I normally loved the peace and quiet on my own, it was always a relief after anything social or big events. Something like this? You'd definitely think so. But right now it just didn't feel quite right.

Suddenly, there was another little twinge at the back of my mind, like a little tickle. Enough to actually make me scratch my head and turn to see if something had touched me. Then I heard it, "By yourself, but never truly alone anymore. Bonded." It was Bridget's voice coming through.

She could sense what I was feeling through the bond? I thought she could only hear my thoughts? I wasn't even trying to reach out to her again right now.

"Not your feelings. But from that it sounds like you're still having a bit of a hard time. I just left so I wanted to send a little reminder." She explained.

At least that made me feel a bit better. Thoughts were one thing, but needing to control what I was feeling because I couldn't control what feelings they knew about —that was too much.

Bridget's voice was gone now though. Just as quickly as she'd reappeared in my mind. And I needed to clean up, get back to my day, and I really needed to take the time to process all of this a little bit better. Wes wouldn't be gone all day.

Thankfully, there wasn't much to straighten up in the office. Once I was done, I took a moment to look around at everything I could be doing—or should be doing... Deciding what to do next.

Why was I trying to be productive? I didn't feel like being productive. I was just distracting myself at this point. I needed to process and as corny as it sounded, I needed to center myself while I had this time alone.

I was trying to take advantage of having the time for more than a simple hot shower.

The more I thought about it, the more I realized, I needed to get out of the house entirely. Staying here, where everything had been happening—what I needed just wouldn't be possible.

Maybe Wes wouldn't mind if I got out for the night. But how could I frame it? Just needing to get out of the space?

Oh, I know! He knew I'd been in a creative rut for weeks now. This is what I needed for creativity. For flow. That was it.

I grabbed my phone ready to type out my message. But wait... Shoot... What if there's no rooms anywhere? I should probably find a place first. Everything would be ruined if nothing was even available. I text him and then what, "Nevermind, just kidding, couldn't find a room for tonight. I'll still be home." No, that would be stupid.

I laughed at my own inner thoughts. Wow, I really did need this.

But, I couldn't just allow myself to not think about what was about to happen. I couldn't enjoy one of the best parts of being around Wes. With him, I could just forget. I could pretend none of this was happening and that our lives were still normal. But that wasn't the case anymore. He just didn't know that yet and I still had to accept it first.

I was getting there... I was getting there.

I sat down and started searching. Surprisingly, there were a few hotels close by, even the nicer ones, that still had rooms available. But I needed one just a little farther away. I didn't want to be five or ten minutes down the road, I didn't mind a short drive in the morning.

One thing, probably one of the only things I missed about my hometown was the long drives I used to take. It was a small town with no street lights, no busy streets, and depending on how early or late it was you could be the only car on the road. I lost that moving to the city.

Back then, I'd be lying if I said it wasn't a bit suffocating in the beginning. I had to get used to it when I first moved here.

Now, having a little drive to a nice hotel—jackpot.

Then I found it, Whispering Willow Lodge. It looked amazingly peaceful, had spacious rooms, and like it would set the perfect tone for the night I needed. Plus, it wasn't crazy expensive for one night. I texted Wes.

"Hey. I was thinking. I think I know what might help that rut I've been in lately."

"Oh yea?" He got back pretty quickly.

"Yea, you're always telling me to get out more and that I stay in the apartment too much. I think you're right." I wanted to start on more of a positive note. He had been telling me this for a while. "So I think I want to go to a new space for the night. Just to get out and be in something new."

"Oh, ok. You want to go spend the night somewhere?" I could tell he was a little confused. It wasn't exactly what he meant when he'd said to get out of the house before.

"Yea, I think it'll just help me clear my head a bit. Being somewhere without a purpose to accomplish other than brainstorming and writing or something." I decided to jump to describing what I'd found, "I already found a room not too far from here. A little rustic, it's spacious, a bit in the woods. It looks cozy. And you can get that quality Bambi time you're always wanting!" I had to laugh at the end. Bambi normally cuddled with me more and he always acted pouty about it.

"If that's what you want to do and you think it'll help... Go for it babe." He was just going with it. What he did half the time I was telling him things I wanted to do. But he did follow up. "It's just for the night?"

"Yes, just one night. I'll be back in the morning."

"Ok, well I love you. I work tomorrow so I'll see you tomorrow. Let me know if you need anything."

I smiled at the phone, "I love you too."

Now I was actually getting excited. I had something to look forward to rather than feeling full of secrets before this dream takeover tonight.

I booked a room and started packing.

I grabbed a small bag, but I needed to make sure I had everything. Crystals included. I didn't want to leave Wes hanging so I got Bambi fed for the night and prepped her breakfast. I even had some quick stuff already put together so I set aside some lunch for him for tomorrow. I thought I was set. Then, I realized, maybe candles? Would the hotel allow that? I could bring some just in case... If they said no, I wouldn't light them. Maybe they could provide other candles if they just didn't want you to use your own, I didn't know. I was rationalizing.

The candles were in the office, where I'd left them earlier today. But now, as I went to get them, a chill ran down my spine just as I crossed the threshold. My eyes darted around the room, landing on the candles on the desk. Then to the drawer that held the flashlight... my whole body trembled. Suddenly I could hear my own heartbeat. Why did I have this sudden urge to take it with me? Why would I want to try using it again?

It was almost like a voice was speaking directly into my mind, telling me I'd regret not taking it. Every instinct was telling me coming into the office and remembering it was a sign... My eyes were locked on that drawer.

I stopped. This pull felt like my intuition, but something was very wrong. This was the one room not protected. Now I was starting to panic. I needed to get out of this room.

I snatched the candles, my computer, and my book, and rushed back to the front door. Closing the office door behind me. I'd reach out to Bridget, but only when this panic settled. When I knew it was clear.

The office was not a safe room and we'd made our plans there. We didn't sense anything or encounter any dark energy earlier but maybe more movement happened at night.

Finally, I could breathe again. The living room and kitchen were fully protected, everywhere Wes and Bambi would be while I wasn't here. My panicked tension slowly released and with it the pull towards that drawer. The urge for the flashlight had disappeared but now my hand was shaking… I'd been clenching my fist so hard to resist and hadn't even realized. I quietly, even in my head, called out to her.

"Bridget?" Barely a whisper, I wondered if it could make it through the bond.

"Yes? Is everything ok?" Oh, thank God.

"Yes, well, I think so. Is it just you?" I wasn't sure how this worked completely yet. If Maia could hear me.

"Yes, yes, just me. You're not quite strong enough yet to reach both of us at one time." Bridget confirmed but added, "I'll teach you as you get stronger, but you only reached out to me this time."

"Ok, well good." I had a sigh of relief. "I'm going to a hotel for the night. Nothing's wrong, just getting out of my own space for everything. But something just happened."

"Ok..." She was waiting.

"I think he's onto something or at least suspicious."

"What happened?" I couldn't tell if she was concerned or considering the possibility.

"I forgot the only room here not protected is the office. I went to grab a couple things and then felt a very sudden, strange urge to grab the flashlight. It was like I was rationalizing it in my brain. When I realized, I panicked and ran out of the room. It's gone now but all I could think was that I'd regret not taking it."

No voice came into my head for a moment.

"Bridget?"

"Are you in a protected room now?"

"Yes, yes, I waited for my mind to clear to make sure before reaching out to you."

"I don't like that. I'm glad you're going somewhere else tonight. Everything's ok." I could tell she was calculating but being careful of what she said, just in case.

"Get to your space and reach out. We're going to try something. For now, you're ok. But you didn't touch the flashlight right?"

"No, I didn't grab it or even touch it, I'm not taking it."

"Good. Don't." I felt the connection slip away. It's become a very interesting feeling. I don't feel the connection being made, a voice that's not my own just comes into my head. But I always feel it lose its grip, like a loud room falling silent suddenly inside your head.

I gave Bambi a quick kiss and pet, the TV was always left on for her and I was on my way. At this point, feeling like I was nearly running out the door.

But everything would be fine. It had to be.

The hotel was just as beautiful in person, rustic but luxurious. The staff had been so kind and luckily had no issues with me bringing my own candles. They had a few guidelines to follow but I could handle that.

My room was on the second floor, which was perfect. I knew all the rooms would have access to the outdoor area that turned into a courtyard space. I didn't really like the idea of a potential glass slider while I was on my own. I always hoped hotels looked at the reservation details when they were selecting the room you'd actually be staying in for these kinds of reasons. Even when you didn't specify over the phone.

On the second floor, I still had the sliding door, but mine led to a quaint little balcony. It was completed with two chairs and a small table. Perfect for a nice coffee and small breakfast. Hopefully tomorrow morning would be nice enough to make use of it.

There was a fireplace in the corner across the room and a large jacuzzi tub on the opposite wall. Oh, I was so excited for tonight. Just seeing this room, with the addition of a king-size bed, this was just what I needed.

"Bridget?" I had made it, she'd asked me to reach out when I did. I wasn't sure what she had in mind but I was keeping up my end. I told her I would.

"Did you make it? Are you somewhere safe?" Her voice came down the bond. She was calm but still had urgency in her tone,

"I think so? I made it to the hotel and I'm in my room." I wasn't sure what she meant by 'safe' now. "I haven't set up the candles yet but I brought them and I'm about to. I do have a pouch of herbs on me though, and my crystals."

"Ok, good." It sounded like she sighed and it actually sent a chill through my brain. God, that was strange! Did that mean the bond was getting stronger?

Before my thoughts could go any further, Bridget appeared next to the bed. I jumped at the sight.

"Oh God, give me a head's up next time." My hand to my chest, catching my breath. "What are you doing here?"

"I'm sorry, I didn't mean the sudden scare. I told you I wanted to try something."

"I thought you meant later or like, through the bond."

"No, I just didn't want anything to risk him potentially following you."

"Following me?"

"Yes. If he's gotten any suspicion, he could've been trying to attach and follow to see what you were up to. Since you were able to connect with one of his spirits already."

"You think that's why I was getting the urge for the flashlight? He was getting in my head? That's why I was wanting to use it... Really, he wanted me to use it?"

"It's possible."

Now I was cursing, How could I be so stupid. I'd almost fallen for it.

"But you didn't." I flashed a look at Bridget, still forgetting she can read my thoughts while she's here.

"Does he know about you? About what you're trying to do or your abilities?"

"I haven't been able to interfere with his plans, so if he does, he's recognized me so far as a non-threat."

"But he's wondering if I'm a threat?"

"I think the reason he's been coming to you is because he sensed what you were before you even learned. He's keeping an eye."

"This just gets better and better." I sat down on the bed, defeated. "I know there's still a lot to do tonight, but my whole point in coming here was to clear my head and try to prepare with some alone time... So... What was it that you wanted to try?"

"Yes, yes, I'm sorry, this should be quick. I just want to make sure everything is safe."

"Ok... What does that mean?"

"I'm going to take a minute—I'll search your mind, the room, and the bond, for any traces of him. Make sure he's not trying to sneak in any pockets."

"Ok, and if there's any sense of him? Or any pockets he could?"

"I should be able to shove it out and put up shields or wards to keep him out."

"Is where I'm at ok? Do you need me to do anything?"

"Lay down for a minute and just relax. Wait for my word and try not to think about anything specifically."

I did as I was told.

"Close your eyes."

I was trying to relax, focus on my breathing. I didn't feel anything. I normally felt her presence when she was in my head. But I held myself back from peeking out... She said on her word, if I did something I could ruin everything. Stop worrying. I wanted to slap myself out of it.

"Done." Jerking me back, my eyes opened. Looking at Bridget.

"Well? Anything?"

"I didn't find any traces of him." She confirmed, "Which is good. But we still shouldn't let our guard down."

"Did you put shields or those wards up?"

"Yes. For the added protection."

"Great." I was nodding, "Why didn't I feel you this time?" I was confused. I'd felt her every time.

"Because I wasn't using the bond." I narrowed my brows.

"How did you… What did you do then?"

"I was feeling it out. It was more of a sensory thing. If he was there I was a little more nervous about him sensing the bond and hiding. I have the ability to sense presences and I can push that out further than just within myself. Through your mind, this place, through everything, without being noticed. It's another reason I'm so sensitive to his presence in The Crypt."

"Interesting." And mentally noted. "Do I have any other abilities?"

"Well, that I don't know yet." Bridget admitted, "We've been very focused on the matters at hand, we've unfortunately been unable to explore more for you. But we can if you'd like to."

"I just want a better understanding of what all this means for me." This was the first time admitting it out loud.

"I completely understand." She seemed like she genuinely did. "You never had a teacher. You didn't grow up knowing about any of this. It's understandable to have questions. Especially when it comes to all you're able to do."

That honestly made me feel so much better. Maia had been so excited every step of the way. I felt a little crazy to be constantly questioning things. It was this constant push and pull in my brain of why wouldn't I want this and the next second, why the hell would I?

But that was one thing tonight was for, although delayed, I could still have that.

"Well, since we've gotten that taken care of, we have a big night ahead. The reason I came was to relax and try to re-center myself. To prepare."

Bridget acknowledged her cue with a nod. "I will leave you to it then. But just know, Aly, even with everything going on, just ask and we can look into your abilities as we go. Once all is said and done, we can make it a regular thing."

Once all was said and done... In other words, if we make it out alive.

"Let's just make it through tonight." I wanted to understand more... I don't know what held me back so much.

Bridget smiled again as she began to fade, leaving me with one more note, "Don't hold yourself back, Aly. You're too powerful for that."

Too powerful? What did that mean? Did she sense something more about me that I didn't know? Why would she leave me with that?

I couldn't let myself start spiraling now though. Tonight was about centering.

I texted Wes to let him know I'd made it to the hotel and that Bambi had already eaten.

Now me. What did I need? What did I want?

I looked over at the jacuzzi. I'd thought about it, but at this point it really felt like more work than relaxing. Lighting candles, ording room service and TV sounded like good wind-down time.

I should order that real quick before I'm too hungry…I grabbed the menu to look for the service desk number. Oh! Oh, it was modern! I scanned the QR code and it popped up the order menu. Oh amazing! Now THIS actually did get better and better.

Scanning the menu I couldn't help but keep glancing at the one candle I'd set on the night stand I hadn't lit yet. I needed to get this order in… But Bridget's words were still lingering in my mind. "Too powerful," that's what she'd called me… Too powerful. But not like I was actually too powerful, but just in a sense of it would be disappointing to see me hold myself back. Or did she mean too powerful? What would that even be?

I shook my head, bringing my attention back to my phone. I just needed this order in and then I could think. Food would also help me think better. I realized now I hadn't eaten for hours.

Sent. Order submitted.

Great, thirty minutes. Perfect.

Ok, back to Bridget... So obviously I'd have to be able to do more than just be able to connect with spirits. It would have to be more. I mean, apparently I can take on the freakin' Grim Reaper!

I looked back at the candle I'd set on the night stand. I hadn't lit anything yet, I was waiting until I was more at a point for meditation. I figured I'd do that at some point.

Obviously, I couldn't fall asleep with them lit so I'd cleanse before... Or should I have candles lit while in the dream? I felt like that wasn't the right choice.

Now I was just going off in my head again. Not the point, not the point. Bridget had mentioned a few things we could even try doing while reconnecting these lost souls... Was that because she could do it for us or she believed I could?

I had planted myself back on the bed to wait for the food. The jacuzzi was too much work and I didn't want to be in a towel or robe when they arrived. Now I looked back at the candle.

If I was so powerful, shouldn't I be able to at least light a candle? How would that work though?

I looked directly at it. Do I just think that I want it lit? Picture it lit? Nothing was happening yet.

"Light" At first I just thought the word. Still nothing.

There had to be something.

Now I was just staring at it. What did I have to do? I felt like Spider-man figuring out his webs for the first time.

Bridget said she pushed out her abilities. Her senses. Could I push out a thought like the bond?

I tried again. I pushed the thought towards the candle, *Light,* and a moment later, it was lit.

It worked.

And I was frozen.

That really just happened. I lit a candle with my mind. I took a breath, soaking in the moment. This was all real. What we were doing was real. The ghosts, The Reaper, the ancestor stories, Bridget, The Crypt, all of it, and I couldn't deny this anymore.

I didn't feel upset that I couldn't deny it. I wasn't even upset that I for sure knew I wasn't going to wake up tomorrow realizing all of this had been the most elaborate dream I'd ever had.

No, my mind was accepting. The tension in my body was releasing. I had been on such a high defensive mode, trying to protect myself and Maia... I needed to talk to Bridget. I wanted to know what more I could do.

Everything was hitting me. Of course, this is what did it... One little candle lights for me and my mind just instantly confirms, "I am more powerful! She's right!" I had to laugh at myself for this one.

But now I needed to know.

Chapter 11

Tonight wouldn't be the right time to bring up my new discovery to Bridget, at least not during the dream. Still, I couldn't help but wonder if this was something else Bridget had been waiting for me to figure out on my own. I mean, I wouldn't even be surprised at this point. Though a little guidance would be nice for once!

I made a face at the wall as if she were still there.

But soon, we'd all be connecting, and I needed to focus. This dream needed my full attention. No distractions. There would be plenty of time to badger her later—and oh would I. Especially if she already knew.

Then I realized... I couldn't be the only one. My eyes grew as the thoughts rushed through my head. What about Maia? If we were both these special descendants, what else could she do?

If she had tried anything, she wouldn't just keep that to herself... She couldn't. Honestly, Maia wouldn't be able to contain herself—not if anything had actually worked. She'd been so excited about connecting with ghosts, the thought may not have even crossed her mind. Not yet anyway.

We could both connect to the other side, but would other abilities be different? And if they were... What would those look like coming together?

Ok, that was enough, I needed to stop. I couldn't let this just consume me now. I needed to get my mind back on track.

Grabbing my phone, I texted Maia, "Almost ready?"

"Yep, just getting into bed." Luckily, she was quick to respond.

"Great, do you have your crystals? Are you cleansing with candles first?"

"Yes to the first, and to the second, do you mean like meditation?"

"Yea, it'd be good to cleanse and meditate. Clear your mind a bit. Especially since this is your first time going in."

"Oh, I guess you're probably right. I didn't think about that. I'll get my candles."

A few moments later, she called.

"Hey, you ok?" Now I was wondering if she was getting cold feet.

"Yea, yea. I'm ok." She sounded hesitant, "You were there once before, when Bridget first came to you... You were ok afterwards, right? When you woke up."

"Oh, yea, I was ok after I woke up. Are you getting nervous, Maia?"

"No... Well... Maybe a little." She admitted, "I just realized this is all getting really serious. It's not a game. We are helping people, but I... I just want to know what it was really like in there."

She finally wanted a glimpse of true understanding and reality before she jumped again. Finally.

I could've been totally honest and told her a bit more, but I knew what she still really needed was a pep talk. She needed to know that she could handle what we were about to do. That she could handle what we were about to experience. I could still be honest, but stay positive at the same time...in a way.

I took a breath, "Honestly, I was really freaked out the last time. But that was because I didn't know where I was, what the place even was, or who Bridget was. It was gloomy and dark and it felt really strange. It was sad to see the spirits, but, you and I will be ok. It was just sad to see so many spirits who had lost their way."

"What do you mean by it feeling strange?"

"I have vivid dreams all the time. This felt like you're in a dream but you can actually feel everything. You can smell the forest, you can feel what you're touching. All your senses are *present*." I had to emphasize that last word. I still couldn't get over how weird that was.

"But, we won't get stuck, right? Like, that's not something that could go wrong. We aren't on a timer or anything once we get there?"

"Oh Maia, no. You don't have to worry about that." I gave a sigh of relief. "No, no, we're not dead yet. We won't get stuck. And we have Bridget, remember. We aren't trying this on our own. We'll stick together and Bridget will be right there with us to make sure everything goes as planned. When we're done, you'll wake up feeling like you've just had the weirdest, most vivid dream in your life."

Finally, Maia sighed, "Ok, that makes me feel a whole lot better. I was getting so nervous. I knew I had to say something. If I didn't, I wasn't sure if the nerves would keep me from being able to actually sleep to even get into the dream."

"Like I said, get your stones and your candles, get set up and in the right head space. Then just text me when you're ready... I promise, everything will be fine."

That is, as long as we don't have a run in with some surprise appearance from our very unwelcome guest.

"Ok, that sounds good. Ok, yea, I'll text you." Maia hung up.

Good grief! I was carrying our whole team.

"Ok, I'm all set. You good?" My phone buzzed to Maia's text, twenty minutes later.

I lingered an extra moment, just staring at her text before reaching to respond.

It was time. There was no backing out now.

We were going back—it would feel the same, but it would be ok. I knew what to expect at least… mostly. I knew what it would feel like, what it would look like. I knew what we were getting into and I would have Maia there with me.

I took one last deep breath and reached for my phone, "I'm good. All set."

Blowing out the candle on the nightstand I'd left lit, I laid down, and closed my eyes. I could already picture the forest—the darkness, the gray mist, the clearing of lost souls, all of it. I felt myself begin to slip under, my mind already taking me there and I released control.

I knew Bridget was waiting to feel us coming. She was waiting to feel our presence to pull all the way under. And here we were.

"Hello Aly. Hello Maia." Bridget's voice rang loud and clear.

I opened my eyes to find us back in the same open field as my first time here. But this time, Bridget hadn't bothered to surround us in darkness first. Probably a better choice with Maia.

"Wow." Maia was standing next to me, hugging her elbows, looking up and around at the looming forest before us.

"Maia, this place, inside these woods, is what I call, The Crypt." Bridget gave me a brief glance as if to say 'don't worry, I won't say too much.'

"This is where the wandering souls reside while their bodies are healing or until they fully cross over."

"They're just wandering around these woods all day?" Maia looked from Bridget to me and back again, "So, they aren't even trying to find their healing body?"

Her confusion was valid. You hear lost soul or wandering spirit and you probably picture spirits searching the earth trying to figure out what's going on. But this wasn't a movie. They weren't walking up to their loved one's saying, "Can you see me?" It apparently didn't work quite like that. Shocker.

"Well, I'm not sure how many of them, if any, are fully aware of their current state. I'm not sure they even know they have bodies healing out in the world still."

"Have you talked to any of them?"

"I have talked to some. When they first arrive they're, of course, a little panicked. They don't know what's going on. I try to ask them about themselves and calm them down. But the longer they're here, the more they forget. The more they forget, the more they simply become wanderers."

"But if they're still here, their human body is still healing? Did you ask the questions because it could help send them back?" Maia glanced at me while she asked, as if sparked with an idea.

"No, at least not that same day. But, I did write down what I learned so I could share my notes with you two. At times they would understand what happened, but unfortunately, their understanding didn't mean their body was able to reconnect on its own. It's just not that simple.

"At first, I thought it might be possible—them finding their way back. But after some time of that not happening, that's when I realized, they needed a bridge. They needed the descendants." Bridget gestured at both of us. We were the bridge they needed.

The bridge. The descendants. Both words carried such weight—neither of which we'd ever heard growing up. But we understood and nodded our acknowledgement to Bridget.

Even if the lost spirits didn't know it, we were their one hope. We couldn't mess this up.

"But we shouldn't waste time. I know you must have many questions but we can get to all of that later. Now we need to move." Bridget gestured for us to follow as she turned towards the opening in the forest wall.

I extended my hand to Maia mouthing, 'It'll be ok.' Maia was still wide eyed, taking everything in. I wondered what she'd think once we were on the inside. This was nothing compared to what we were about to go into.

She took one more look at the forest and released her crossed arms to take my hand.

"You were right about the creepy forest. Jesus, these poor souls. Poor Bridget for being stuck here."

I had to smirk, "Told you."

I squeezed her hand, reassuring as I followed Bridget to that dark opening once more, now with Maia in tow.

All those past sensations I had told Maia about came flooding back as we stepped off the grass of the open field and onto that dirt path, crossing through the small opening. Crossing into the forest was like willingly being swallowed by darkness. I hoped I'd never need to get used to this feeling.

The musky smell, the chill running up your arms, and again, that strange ability to feel everything you touched. Nothing had changed.

I looked back at Maia. She was still wide-eyed, looking everywhere, at everything around us.

"You ok?" I whispered.

She met my eyes then, realizing I was looking at her. "Yea, I'm fine. I... I guess I wasn't expecting it to feel so real." She looked around again, "I know what you said, but I don't really know, I still wasn't expecting... This."

I smirked, trying to keep it a little light-hearted, "Yea, imagine my first time." I gave a little laugh at my own traumatic experience. At least this was more bewilderment for Maia. I didn't know where the hell I was or what the hell was going on the first time I was here.

I turned back, continuing to follow Bridget. We were almost to the clearing now. I could see it now, faintly over the tops of the brush, almost like a city skyline in the woods.

We didn't necessarily have a full-fledged plan of what was supposed to happen or how this would work. We weren't sending anyone back from here... We couldn't. But we did need to talk to them, learn about them, and Bridget was moving like she was on a mission. So hopefully that meant she had something up her sleeve.

We were going to the same place we'd gone the first time I'd been here. The small hidden area, behind a patch of bushes just before the clearing. The perfect spot to keep us hidden from anyone on the other side, while also providing us full visibility when we wanted to peek through the bushes.

Luckily, it wasn't too long of a walk from the forest's entrance.

But Bridget didn't stop once we made it there. She walked straight up to the brush that lined the edge of the clearing and peered over the top. Scanning.

I followed, Maia right behind me.

"There's so many more than I expected... Do they all just stay in that one area?" Maia asked as she peered over the bush.

"They wander into the woods too, but this is where they all first arrived. I think it brings some comfort to be around the others."

"That makes sense. Sad, but makes sense. I guess I'd rather be in there then wandering these woods by myself endlessly." As soon as the words left my mouth I regretted it. That's exactly what Bridget had been doing before we came around. She'd known why she was here and what was going on, yet could do nothing about it.

I subtly glanced to where she stood at my side, reached out, and grabbed her hand. She looked surprised at the touch but looked up at me.

I'm sorry, I mouthed when her eyes met my face. This was the first time I saw tears in her eyes. Even in the little time knowing her, I knew she wouldn't let those tears out, but this was clearly difficult for her.

"I haven't felt physical touch like this in years. I don't even remember the last time."

This was about more than just the spirits. She wanted to help them, but she also needed out of this hell. She didn't want to escape and just leave them behind though. That's what the tears were. Years of sadness and now her freedom at her fingertips but she wouldn't leave them behind.

I gave a sympathetic smile and whispered, "We'll get you out of here. We'll get you all out of here."

"Right, let's just focus on them first." I nodded in return and let her hand go.

She hadn't even done anything wrong and yet, it seemed like she was still trying to redeem herself. Or maybe it was the healer in her that just felt the inclination to help.

"So who is it? How do we talk to them?" Maia's voice brought our attention back to the clearing.

"Yes, she's right over there, by the pond. Her name's Maddie." Bridget pointed in the direction of the pond, "Now, we don't want to scare her or cause any nerves. So we're all going in and I will introduce you both."

"We're *all* going over there?" *Umm, excuse me? Was she serious?* I was blinking at Bridget as if I had heard her incorrectly.

"We need to act like you're both new here and should be making friends." Bridget clarified, "I fear, if it's only me, it might feel like an interrogation. That could just scare her off."

I couldn't hide my surprise. Although it made more sense to go to her, it didn't mean I wanted to do it. I had pictured Bridget bringing her to us, in this spot, not us going out into the open...

"Do you think she'll buy that?"

"As long as you both stay calm and ask what you need to in a way that sounds like you're just getting to know her, I think it'll be fine. Even spirits need friends, especially here."

Maia took a breath beside me and squeezed my hand. "Aly, we can do this."

I raised a brow at her, when did she get so confident to be in a sea of ghosts?

"We need her name and where she's from, or where she lived, right? That's what's important." Her voice wasn't even shaking, "Anything else would be a bonus."

I narrowed my eyes at her slightly. Maybe she realized if she was here now, she had to be ready to jump and go all in. She wanted to show she wouldn't hesitate. I admired it, honestly.

I looked from her to Bridget and shot a thought directly into Bridget's mind. "If anything starts to go south, you've got this?"

She nodded.

I took a breath, nodded at Maia, still holding her hand. Then looked back at Bridget, "Ok, so where's the entrance?"

The entrance wasn't too far from where we already were, but my feet got heavier with each step. Maia gripped my hand tighter, even as both our palms became clammy. We knew what we had to do, we weren't ready, but we weren't stopping.

The woods were dark and gray, with plenty of places to hide. Almost too many. It made you feel invisible. Needing to step out into this clearing felt like an unveiling. Like we were putting ourselves on full display for anyone watching. But we were here, we may not have been on a real timer, but we were still on a timer. You never knew when *he* might show up. It was now or never.

"Ready girls?" Bridget paused just before the opening to the clearing, looking at both Maia and I. Waiting for confirmation.

Sharing a quick glance, I squeezed Maia's hand once more reassuring and nodded. "Let's do this."

With one last smile and deep breath, Bridget beckoned us to follow her through the tree veil into the clearing.

It was like seeing a whole other side of The Crypt. Being on the outside, looking in, was one thing. You got an understanding of it. You could see most of it. But now, standing right on the edge, almost felt like an entirely new place.

Other than a couple stone tables, benches, and a pond with a small fountain on the other end, the land was bare. The sky was still cloudy and gray, giving off only slightly more light than the woods. It looked like an abandoned park that even the birds or squirrels forgot existed.

The only relief was that no one seemed to care when we entered. Not one spirit looked up from what they were doing.

Which really wasn't much of anything—what mattered is that they didn't care enough to look up. We went completely unnoticed.

We were only paused for a brief moment before Bridget led us in the direction of the pond, where Maddie was sitting. She was staring at the water, her eyes lost in a daze, as if watching the fish that were no longer there. She'd probably still toss in food if she had any.

As we got closer, Bridget gently greeted the girl, hoping not to startle her, "Maddie?"

She didn't jump or react. Simply perked up at her name, blinking out of her trance, and slowly looked up. Seeing Bridget, her face softened and she smiled.

"It's been a while Bridget, hello." Maddie reached out her hand.

Accepting the greeting and taking her hand, Bridget turned toward us, "These are some newcomers. They're still getting themselves acquainted around here, but you know how unnerving it can be when you first arrive. I thought they could use a new friend to feel a bit more comfortable."

"Hello," Maddie looked at both of us. She was smiling but you could see a weariness in her face.

She didn't necessarily look tired, as if she hadn't been sleeping—I wasn't sure sleep was even a thing around here. It didn't seem like it would be. Ironically, it was more like her spirit was draining... This must be what it looked like. This must be what it looked like when they were beginning to slip away. Not just because of this place, she was tired of hanging on in general... This was part of how Bridget knew she was close. She not only sensed it, you could see it on her face.

We needed to find her human form fast.

"Hi Maddie, it's lovely to meet you." I put on my biggest smile, "Though I wish it were under better circumstances." Thankfully that got a laugh. I wasn't sure what time period she was from, but I figured a little more formal was the better route to go.

"I'm Aly and this is my sister, Maia."

"Oh, how tragic. Sisters here at the same time." She gave a sympathetic look.

"Tragic, but kind of poetic isn't it?" Bridget piped in.

"Tragic, poetic, it was Maia's fault, but we don't need to get into that." Maia gaped her mouth at my blaming remark and rolled her eyes.

"Anyway," laughing at my own joke and Maia's reaction, I continued, "We were just surprised when Bridget told us there could be someone else from where we're from in here. Bridget said memories do get fuzzy in here after a while... But do you maybe remember where that was? Where you're from?"

We had no idea where she was actually from but clearly she knew Bridget. She could have told Bridget in the past. She may not remember where, but it wouldn't be suspicious to think she could've told Bridget when she'd first arrived.

"Oh my, it has been a while. Bridget is correct, my memory is not very good anymore."

"That's ok. Umm... Maybe there's certain things you do remember about that place? We might be able to help."

We'd all taken a seat on the benches now to join her around the pond. It would've been awkward to just stand there, staring down at her. Now that would've felt like an interrogation... "Where are you from? What's your name?" We weren't the ghostbusters.

Maddie took a moment. I crossed my ankles and put my hands in my lap, not to add any pressure. Something about the look she had while she was thinking... She wasn't concerned or upset, she actually looked like she wanted to remember. She wanted back what was forgotten.

"I don't remember what happened to me. But I remember a lot of woods, a lot of hiking, and the smell of the trees. Oh I don't know where it was... But I don't think I could ever forget that smell." She closed her eyes like she could still smell them, "They had more pokey branches, like green needles."

As she was recalling those memories I could already see her features changing just the slightest. Like a bit of light was fighting to creep back in. Then it hit me like a ton of bricks.

It wasn't just her outer body not healing fast enough that kept her here. It wasn't just this place keeping her hidden and tucked away. It was the isolation it created. The hopelessness. If she thought she was already dead, there would be no point fighting it! These spirits may not be able to heal themselves, but if they're fighting to come back, creating that bridge could be easier!

This could be it.

We needed to help these spirits know they could fight it.

Maybe they just needed to know what to do. Frankly, we needed to know what they could do too.

And with her description, I was already pretty sure I knew where she was talking about now.

"The only other thing I can remember is a big sign, I think it said... Evergreen on it?"

I gave her a big smile, "I think I know where that is."

"Really? It's all still very fuzzy."

"That's ok, everything you described sounds very familiar. It actually does sound like where Maia and I are from."

Maddie looked relieved, like she was happy she'd done something right, she'd been helpful. This poor thing.

"So where is that? Where are you from dear?"

"We're from Washington, and I think you are too Maddie."

"Huh, I don't know what that is or where that is, but it sounds delightful."

Her positivity made me and Maia both giggle, "It really is Maddie. It's just as you described."

Oh, this poor, sweet woman did not deserve this place.

Now Maia spoke up, we still needed her name, "Now, we don't mean to keep you, I know this is probably a strain that we'll also understand better after some time. But just real quick, I've always loved the name Maddie, what's yours short for?"

She smiled at the compliment, "Madelyn, my name is Madelyn Bennett."

"Madelyn Bennett, that's very pretty. I like that." Maia smiled at her.

I glanced around to see if anyone had begun to stir. I wasn't trying to make any commotion or look out of place with this new interaction. But anyone who could've noticed remained unbothered and only focused on themselves.

"You've been so nice to us, maybe we can see if we can help you out with more later if you'd like to try and remember anything. Maybe clear a blindspot or two. If we hopefully can see you again soon?"

"Yes! Please, I'm usually right over here by the pond."

"Thank you for taking some time for new friends Maddie. I should help them continue to get settled in for now." Bridget gently touched her shoulder as we all got up and began to leave.

"Oh, my pleasure, please come around again soon."

"Will do." Bridget gave her shoulder a little squeeze before we turned back towards the exit.

I really thought that would be a lot scarier... We were speaking to ghosts... face to face. Not with a tool, a flashlight, or anything. They were sitting right in front of us. If they wanted to touch us we would've been able to feel it. But there wasn't even a touch of unease or tension. Just sweet Maddie and a bunch of spirits minding their business. They weren't trying to hurt us. I don't know which one it was, but one had already tried to make a connection in the real world. The only ones we hadn't seen yet were the other witches here... I still didn't know where they stayed most of the time.

Yet, now, I had a strange feeling. Only as we were leaving. I wasn't physically ill, but something felt off. It wasn't any sense from the spirits around us, it was something about this place suddenly. This had gone almost too well, too easy. Was I just being paranoid now? This feeling wasn't there before... But now... Something was happening.

There had been a shift and it felt dark. I was trying to convince myself it was just paranoia but then my intuition was telling me it was stupid to convince myself not to listen to my gut... which also seemed obvious.

It felt like eyes were watching our every move. The other spirits around us were still paying no attention to us. Not one had even looked up. Could this be how it felt when a new spirit was arriving? Was *he* here?

I was still walking towards our exit. Looking around everything seemed normal. But something was wrong.

We had just nearly made it back to safety, outside the clearing, or as safe as it could be here really, when Bridget suddenly stopped. Still looking around, I nearly smashed into her.

"What is it? What's wrong?" I snapped my head back and around to look in any direction. Was my feeling right?

Bridget turned to face me and her look said all I needed to know,

"It's not Maddie is it?"

"No. Not Maddie. But I need to get you both out. Now."

Chapter 12

Launching forward, I sat straight up. I was back in bed, back at the hotel, now gasping for air. Looking around I realized where I was and calmed.

God, was this what it would be like every time? Every time I went back to that place, if I had to go back? I wasn't sure if I could handle that... This felt like death. Or being brought back to life I guess?

Catching my breath there was still a slight pain in my chest, but it was easing. It was like my own soul went to the Crypt in those dreams and then shoved its way back in. I'd felt it the last time too. Could that have been what it was—or was I losing my mind for real now? I hadn't really given it a second thought, just assumed it was the pain of catching my breath. Now, it had me curious.

Still trying to collect myself I hadn't even noticed Bridget in the corner yet, waiting for me to recover.

"Are you ok?" she asked.

Jumping slightly, finally noticing her presence. "Oh geez, I didn't know you'd come back with me."

"Apologies."

"Well, I'm a lot better than the first time you brought me in there." I put a hand on my chest, "Is Maia ok? She got back alright? Did you check on her first?"

"Yes, she's ok. She's getting her bearings together. Coming out was a little more difficult for her first time, but she's ok."

"Ok, good." That was a relief. I didn't really care about my own reaction. After my first Crypt visit I knew I'd be fine.

"I told her we would reach out once you came out. Give her a little extra time and I think we need to talk first."

"Yea. We do. What the hell happened in there? What was that?" I'd collected myself and was coming back to that strange feeling right before Bridget rushed us out.

"It was him." Bridget pushed herself off the wall, "I felt him coming. I needed to get you both out, like I promised."

"But who was he coming for? I thought you said it wasn't for Maddie? We were talking to her because she was the closest one to losing touch with her body." I was so confused. He only came when he was taking a soul. If there wasn't one to take yet, why would he show up.

"She is the closest, but no, he wasn't there for her." Bridget scratched her head and began pacing, "I was worried this might happen but I wasn't sure it would."

"Worried what would happen?" I was staring at her now. Expecting. But nervous.

"After you called out to me, before you came here, I got a suspicion. I guess it's been confirmed now... He's become too suspicious of your interest in these spirits. He was trying to figure out the plan. I think he's tracking you." Bridget stopped pacing to look at me.

"Tracking me? I'm being hunted by The Reaper now?"

"It's possible."

"For what?" I nearly yelled it, throwing my hands up exasperated. "This just keeps getting better and better. I'm not even dead yet, what can he do to me?"

Shit, I needed to calm down... I just yelled, I'm not even dead yet and asked what someone could do to me. I'm in a freaking hotel room and no one else can see the ghost witch I'm speaking to... I'd look and sound insane to anyone who walked by, heard from a nearby room, or knocked. Last thing I need right now is some friendly neighbor calling in a wellness check.

Closing my eyes and taking a breath to calm myself down, I looked at Bridget again. Her patience was showing, I could tell she could practically read my thought process on my face.

She gave me a look and raised a brow. Taking a breath, I nodded.

"I'm not positive why, but I think he's suspicious because he's seeing you as a potential threat to his supply now. To the spirits in his Crypt."

No... This was actually making sense.

"I've been trapped there for so long," She continued, "and I've never been able to do anything. I haven't been a threat yet."

"So, he's trying to kill me? Stop me? How does he stop me? Would he even know or do you think he's also trying to figure that out?"

"That part he might be trying to figure out, but I think I know what he's trying to do or would do."

I just looked at her, waiting, "Care to share?"

"I was getting there," shifting her eyes and putting her hand up in defense, "He can't physically kill you and he's too impatient to wait... I think to stop you, all he can do is try to trap you like I am. I think he came to The Crypt with the intention of not allowing you to leave."

My jaw dropped, "He can do that?" My eyes started darting around the room as if searching for an answer. "What do we do then? I mean, I know we can keep that from happening, we must be able to, but I have a feeling tonight won't be the last time I need to go into that place."

"Yes, we can prevent it. We will prevent it. I won't let it happen." Bridget made a motion with her hands as if to say, 'We can just breathe.'

"We made it through tonight. We got answers we needed. I think we need to call Maia to discuss some things now. And I know we've been wary of saying anything too early, but I think it's time she should know."

"About The Reaper?" I gave her an incredulous look. Why did me being hunted mean we needed to tell Maia now?

"Yes Aly, if he's tracking you, he could start tracking her too. We need to take precautions and she needs to be careful. After tonight, don't you think you might be underestimating her a little bit?"

Well, God, she didn't need to call me out like that.

"I've been trying to keep it more positive for Maia. She's been so excited about everything, I haven't wanted to ruin that or scare her."

"I understand, but this could involve her more now too. You said you didn't want to say anything until it was necessary." She paused just a moment to remind me with a look, "Well... It's time. It's necessary."

"Fine." I gave up. She was right. It could be dangerous at this point not to. "We'll give her a call, reach out, see how she's feeling, and after we debrief, we can explain."

"Good. Deal. Now call." Bridget pointed at the phone then crossed her arms to wait.

"Hello?" Maia's voice came through the phone speaker.

"Hey, Maia, you ok? It's Aly…. Don't worry, this is real. We're back now."

A loud sigh came through the phone.

"Oh that was insane! You weren't kidding in the slightest!"

"No, no I wasn't." I couldn't help but chuckle at her comment, "But I know it can take a minute to feel normal again… Do you need any more time before we debrief with Bridget?"

"Um, yea, that might be a good idea. I've pulled myself together and I'm starting to feel ok, but maybe just another couple minutes." She paused a moment, but she had something else to say, "But, before you hang up. Umm… When Bridget was taking us back and getting us out… I didn't snap out right away. It felt like I was traveling through a brief darkness before I was back and waking up. I don't know if that's normal, but then also, during those few moments, I heard a man's voice. It was deep and kind of muffled, but he knew my name."

Bridget and I looked up from the phone, staring at each other, wide-eyed.

"I just wanted to mention it before I forgot. But you're right. I need to collect myself a little more, a bit better, and call you back in a few."

"Ok, ok. Take your time Maia. We'll talk through it all." That was all I could push out through my shock. The phone clicked as Maia hung up and I just slowly dropped the phone to the bed.

"We checked on him tracking me... We didn't even think about Maia beforehand." Shit. "We need to go check over there... Now. Before we debrief."

"I'll stay discreet." With that, Bridget disappeared. She shouldn't be gone long, she couldn't be. She needed to stay hidden from Maia and all of that combined would take a lot of her strength.

I hoped Maia took everything well. We weren't trying to hide anything from her, it was just a matter of if she needed to worry about something or not. Unfortunately, now the threat was growing rather than us successfully continuing to avoid it. How could he have gotten so far ahead of us so quickly? We needed to find out if Maia had also tested out any other ability like I had. Could he have sensed it?

Bridget reappeared moments later.

"Ok. So far, no trace of him and wards are up. I remained out of sight and out of her mind, so Maia didn't notice a thing. She'll know everything only once she calls back."

"And are you ok?" I looked at her, I was gaining the understanding of the strain this took.

"I was able to finish fast enough to return without losing too much strength and I'll have time to build it back, it doesn't take too long luckily, I'll be ok now."

Bridget took a seat on the bed, confirming what I wasn't sure was possible, and we waited.

This was the worst part—the waiting. I was not ready for this call to even happen. I was ready for the debrief, just not everything else that came with it. But the waiting was torture. It always was. No matter what you didn't want to do, this is the part that gets your stomach in knots.

First, it should all be easy, we're just talking about the next steps, where we went from here. Obviously, I wasn't too nervous about that. But The Reaper? How were we supposed to introduce that topic, that entity, to Maia?

Before I could even try to think more, try to come up with some sort of idea, the phone buzzed and Maia's name lit up the screen.

I swore instantly, looked at Bridget, and accepted the call.

"Hey Maia, are you all set now?"

"Hey, yea. I think I'm ready to go now. So, um, what's first?"

I looked at Bridget for direction. She nodded, accepting me passing the lead.

"Well first, do you both feel like you were able to gather enough information from Maddie?" Bridget's voice came down the bond.

"We got her name, we know where she's from, and this is probably around where she was when she got hurt. So I think so. At least enough to research and connect the dots." I looked at the phone, "What'd you think Maia? You asked her name but you seemed pretty satisfied with the info too."

"Uh, yea. We should have enough to go on… I do have a question though… This might sound weird though."

I narrowed a brow, "What do you mean?" What is it?"

"Bridget, are you able to bring any items back here from the forest? From The Crypt?"

Bridget and I both looked at each other confused.

"Yes, actually. I was going to give you both the notes I've collected over the years from the spirits arriving. I hoped it would help in finding them. What are you looking for exactly?" She paused, then looked nervous, "Does this have anything to do with that voice you heard coming out?"

"No, no. It's actually about while we were talking to Maddie. It's just kind of a hunch." She sighed. Did she think we were going to think she was crazy? After everything?

"Maia, whatever it is, we're already talking about lost souls, guiding them back to their earthly bodies, witches, a limbo world called The Crypt, and we were just in it inside our dreams. I don't think you need to worry about us thinking you're crazy or something is just too far-fetched at this point."

Maia laughed, "Ok, fair."

Bridget smirked at the full list.

It all sounded crazy, but here we were!

"Ok, well, when we were talking to Maddie, as she was describing where she lived and what she remembered, I kept feeling this pull. I even noticed as she was trying to remember, a little bit, even just the slightest, of light came back into her face and eyes. I was being pulled. I'll just say it. It almost felt like her body was trying to call out to me or pull me to find her. Like she could sense me and knew I could help, but I couldn't figure out the direction."

"Oh my." Bridget's eyes were huge when I looked up, "Maia."

Was she excited? What did this mean?

"Maia, I think you have the gift of tracking! Oh goodness. You needed an anchor piece."

"Gift of tracking? Anchor piece?" We both asked at the same time.

"Yes, yes. This makes you both even stronger as a bridge. And, it will be much easier to find these spirit's bodies."

"What does that mean though? I'm like search and rescue?"

"I'm not sure what that is, that's after my time. But I will get you the anchors! What this means is that you, neither of you need to be physically present to help bridge the gap."

"Maia doesn't need to physically track down the people? So she just has to locate them in her mind?"

"Precisely. It's very similar to when I brought the three of us together in our minds. I can get an item from the spirit in The Crypt, then Maia can let the item lead her mind to that person's body and we can connect them."

"Damn, so I'm like powerful?" Maia sounded shocked but also like she was doing a hairflip. I couldn't help but chuckle.

"This is an amazing gift Maia. I can't wait to see what more you both can do."

I couldn't even imagine what 'more' looked like at this point. But, I couldn't lie either, the farther we got wrapped up in this mess I couldn't help but get more and more curious. I mean I also lit a freaking candle with my own mind too. What *would* be next?

"Ok, now as exciting as all this is, and I will get you whatever you need Maia, we do have a couple other things to talk about."

Damn—I'd almost forgot. I wished we had.

"The voice you heard. I think I know what and who it was, and unfortunately, it's not good."

Bridget looked at me before continuing. Confirming I wanted her to begin the explanation or to let me jump in to explain.

I knew I could let her explain, but now I felt like a chicken. I thought I was protecting Maia but she needed to know. I've known everything, Bridget told me and it was my choice to keep hidden, I should be the one to tell Maia now. Bridget was here to clarify or confirm. But this was on me.

"So... What was that?" Maia was waiting.

"What exactly did that voice say to you?" I just wanted to know first. I also kind of thought it was a good lead in.

"It was a man's voice, like I said, a deep voice, and he said, 'Hello Maia, I've been looking for you.'"

Looking for us. Great.

"Maia... There's a couple things you need to know." I was so nervous, why was I so nervous about her reaction? I needed to stop underestimating her.

"Do you know who that voice was?" Her voice was shaking slightly.

I took a breath and went for it, "These lost souls we're helping—we're helping them because they were never meant to end up in that place. The Crypt was created for and only ever meant to be for the witches of Salem until we came along."

"Oh my God. What happened? Why are they going there then?"

"Well that's why we're helping. Somewhere down the road, it was discovered and basically taken over. Now, The Crypt is being run by The Reaper and he is stealing souls as they die." I practically spit the last part out just to get it out. "We're trying to help these people find themselves again before The Reaper can take them."

"Holy shit."

"Yea. And now... Uh, well he's caught onto something, some part, of what we're doing or who we are and now we're a threat to him. So he's hunting us. We think that voice you heard... It was him." I finally let out a breath.

"Is that everything?" Maia asked.

"Oh, and I can light a candle and snuff it out with my mind. Yea that's everything." Might as well get it all out now.

Bridget perked at the last part, looked at me, and clapped with a giddy smile, mouthing 'we'll practice that later!'

"So, um...ok. That's a lot. I guess we're starting with finding people but that just got a bit harder if someone's hunting us... And you said The Reaper? Like, as in The Grim Reaper?”

“The one and only. Yea, I know, that was my reaction too.”

“Great, great. Well, what do we do now?”

“Well a lot of things have been changing so that’s what we’re figuring out now. But later... Basically I have to help Bridget kill The Reaper and destroy The Crypt.”

Now Maia went silent.

Then Bridget took the opportunity to speak, “And now, Maia, with your newly found ability—we may need your help too.”

Chapter 13

I stared at Bridget in shock. What just came out of her mouth? Was I hallucinating?... She did not just suggest Maia's help in our final plan. This conversation was about planning, our next steps, locating spirits, and how to protect ourselves in the process. Not joining the team!

"No. What are you talking about?" I shot the thought straight down the bond, directly at Bridget.

"We don't need to worry about any of that now though. Obviously, there are larger matters at hand." Oh, now she's backpedaling, but only a little—she didn't take it back fully.

Maia still fell silent on the other end of the phone. Nothing came over the bond either.

"Maia?" I asked gently, making sure she was still there.

"Yes, sorry, I'm still here. This is just a lot."

Yea, no kidding.

"You're fine. You don't need to worry about future plans for The Reaper. Just focus on what we're doing now."

"But at the end of all this, once we save these spirits, the end goal is to get rid of The Reaper and that place?" Maia was pushing. She wasn't letting it go.

"Yes, that's the end goal. That's what we need to do." Bridget confirmed.

This shouldn't even be a topic of conversation. I was glaring at Bridget now.

"If that needs to happen—if that's the only way to get these people out and keep anyone else from ending up in that wretched place... I'm in."

"You're in?" I looked at the phone in shock.

"I'm in. I don't know what I can do, but if you think I can help. I'll help how I can."

Great.

"Ok, well, we aren't even at that point yet. So we should probably be focusing on what's going on now." I looked at Bridget to get back on topic.

"Apologies. Yes, you're right Aly. That is a problem for another day."

"Wait…" Maia jumped back in.

No, God, please no.

"Before we got onto all of that, we were talking about the voice I heard when I was waking up. You said you think that was The Reaper?"

Oh, thank God, this actually was back on track.

"Yes—unfortunately. So far that's the only explanation I have for it."

"So he's not just hunting or searching for us. He's already found us."

Silence fell over the room.

"Hunting is a bit of a strong word." Bridget spoke up first, "He's become aware of you both. He's keeping an eye on you."

I just raised a brow at Bridget.

"Ok, keeping an eye… Do we know how he even noticed us—what could've tipped him off? Also, how does he even stop us if he sees us as a threat?" Maia paused, I knew she'd have a lot of questions, but then, "Wait, how did he already know my name?"

Until this moment I'd completely forgotten that while explaining everything, I'd left out a crucial detail. Honestly, I'd really forgotten it completely. There was a lot going on. And I didn't think of that way anymore.

"Maia, I think he's known who we are for at least a little while now."

"What do you mean? Someone else who's known about us? Bridget was waiting for us—Has he been waiting for us?"

"I don't know if he's been waiting for us exactly. But, do you remember that first night, just a couple weeks ago, when we connected to that dark energy? Then it came back later?"

"Oh. My. God. Was that him?"

"I think he's been keeping an eye on us—waiting to see what we might turn into. Or see if we'd finally figure ourselves out."

"Shit! Oh, I just got chills!" It was a rare occurrence to hear Maia curse.

"I know."

"So we were just inviting him in all willy nilly, all because we were frustrated he didn't really want to answer questions." Maia's tone was shifting, from concerned and questioning to strategic and planning. "Ok, so what do we do? We can't just stop, obviously, so how do we avoid the tracking or mask ourselves, or whatever. What's next?"

I knew I'd been a little overprotective so far when it came to Maia, but I was loving this side of her.

Bridget's voice came down the bond at her question, "There are a few things—and we've already begun setting some in place. However, we thought he was only tracking Aly so we started there." Bridget put a finger to her temple, "That's probably why he came to you Maia."

"Has he already done something? Aly?" Now Maia sounded more concerned for me. She'd faced something small—he hadn't done anything to her though.

"I came to a hotel tonight. Not because of him, but I just wanted to get away. He was trying to follow me."

"Trying? So he can't follow?"

"He apparently isn't attached to me like that, so he can't without an object he's connected to."

"The flashlight!"

"The flashlight... He wanted me to bring it with me."

"Did you hear him too?"

"No, he didn't directly speak to me. When I was getting ready to leave—I'll be honest, it's hard to explain. He got into my head somehow... I went into the office to grab a couple things and I just felt something. I didn't know why, but I really wanted the flashlight. I felt like I needed it. But then everything felt very off and I didn't know why I had that feeling so I freaked and ran out. I called out to Bridget and left."

"So was he technically in my head too? Since I was still in the dream?"

Bridget was staring blankly at the bed, as if into a void.

"Technically, I guess, yes." I looked from the phone to Bridget, "Bridget? Are you ok?"

Bridget slowly looked up at me from the bed and I could tell whatever was about to come down the bond was only coming to me.

"He's becoming more dangerous than even I suspected. Once we get some safety measures in place, I think we might need some reinforcements."

Whatever she meant by that, I didn't know. But even Bridget looked scared. I'd seen Bridget concerned and worried, but scared? That was a new one. I didn't like it.

If she said reinforcements, we'd have reinforcements, whatever that meant.

"Ok, so if we're just looking into some things for now and you're getting that item from Maddie, what can we do before we do anything?" Maia broke the silence, bringing our attention back. "Also, you said you've already done some safety measures?"

"Yes, right now there are wards safeguarding both of you and your homes. I wanted to protect the spaces you've already used to communicate."

"You did?"

"I stayed hidden as to not scare you. Basically think of it like those herbs you've been using, just a hundred times over."

"Why would you have scared me?"

Bridget glanced at me, smirked and said, "I tend to give your sister a bit of a jump-scare when I just appear out of nowhere."

Good save. Very funny Bridget.

I rolled my eyes, "Well as far as I'm aware, just like those wards, Bridget can do the same to our minds."

"Really? How does that work?" Maia was intrigued now.

"Yes, yes, it's not a permanent thing though, only temporary. It can feel like a slight tickle but kind of like a temporary tattoo on your mind that creates a wall barrier. No one can enter."

"Would I not even hear you? Don't I need to let people enter for all this to work?"

"There are different ones we're able to use. The one we would use would only allow who you allow to enter."

"So because we're bonded I've already allowed you."

"Exactly."

"Ok, and when I connect with the spirit's anchored item I can allow them to enter just focusing with that?"

"Yes, yes, exactly."

"Well that seems pretty simple. Granted, as simple as tonight can get."

I gave a heavy exhale and laughed, "Right."

"So... Is that everything or is there any other world potentially ending news or steps we need to take?"

I looked at Bridget who shook her head, "No, I think it's finally time for research now and getting ready to come back together."

"Alright! One, two, three break?" Maia laughed, I had to laugh too.

"Ok, get some sleep, I know I need it too. We'll talk in the morning."

The phone clicked and I immediately glared at Bridget. "What were you thinking?"

"Aly, you heard what she said. He's not just coming after you. There's a real danger here, and honestly, we could use all the help we can get. You underestimate her." Bridget shrugged and crossed her arms, as if challenging me to tell her she was wrong.

"I'm not underestimating anything. I was trying to keep her out of the danger. Do you think this part is fun for me?" I shot my arm out like the room before us displayed everything we'd been going through.

"I never said that."

"Good. Because at this point, most of this—this bullshit —isn't fun at all." Now I was fuming, "I didn't ask for this either. I didn't ask to be a bridge, I didn't ask to be needed to battle the damn Grim Reaper, I didn't ask for powers I barely understand, and now I'm just trying to protect my own. Maia is all I have."

"Look. I am sorry. I understand how you feel. You want to protect her. But have you even thought that maybe the best way to do that is to give her the same chance you've had? Neither of you grew up knowing who you truly are or what you're capable of. Think how much better of a position we'd all be in right now if you had gotten to have a mentor like I did. I wasn't allowed to make myself known or tell you anything until you began discovering things for yourself...." She raised a brow and tilted her head slightly, "Sounding familiar?"

Dammit Bridget. I hated when she started making sense like this... Was I now doing that to Maia, basically all over again?

The realization shook me. "Wow—You're right." It must have been written on my face based on Bridget's simple reaction.

"Yea, I know." She closed her eyes and nodded softly.

"Well what do I do then?"

"Nothing. Just keep doing what we've been doing. We won't keep things from Maia anymore and you let her help where she can and wants to."

I couldn't help my slight reluctance before answering, my body tensing at her words, but still, I nodded in agreement.

"You're right... Fine. I'll do better."

"Plus, Maia is in this now. You can't be too focused on her or stopping her from doing something that it could hurt everything."

I threw my hands up in defense, "Hey, I said I'd do better. I admitted I have a problem, that's step one." Holding up one finger on each hand with a nod for emphasis.

"Then I'll leave you to your research and getting some rest. I have an anchor to retrieve now." But just before she vanished, she stopped, "One more thing—if I'm going to be around to train you two, you're going to have to teach me what these things mean... Step one? Search and rescue? These things mean nothing to me." And with that she was gone.

Thankfully she was gone before she could hear me laughing. That's what she was saying to Maia about it being after her time. Oh, poor Bridget.

I did need to start on that research though. We learned that Maia can track people, ideally with the use of a personal item. But, it would still probably be helpful to learn anything we could. Maybe that poor girl is still healing somewhere around here.

Obviously, I'm not trying to go to the hospital now to make the connection. We hadn't even come up with a way to be undetectable to do that. And what, if we had to do that, The Reaper's just going to show up at a hospital full of people? Oh, hell no. But any leads we could find should be helpful. At least to guide us.

Opening my computer, still sitting on my bed, I caught a glance of the time. Food!

With so much going on, I couldn't even remember the last time I'd eaten today. Maybe not since breakfast. I hadn't even left this bed since Bridget appeared in the room. Adrenaline kept the thoughts of food away—until now.

"Trash TV, food, and focus. That's what I need." I said to literally no one but myself, and a burger sounded so good. Especially one from a nicer restaurant. Somehow those were always the best. Hole-in-the-wall pizza and nice restaurant burgers. I don't know why that was but, oh, my mouth watered just thinking about it.

Ready to order, I snagged the phone from the bedside table and the room service menu.

"Wait, what?" My hand was left hovering mid-air over the phone keys. There was no number labeled for room service. Did I have to go downstairs to wait for pickup? This nice of a hotel—there had to be room service.

I flipped around the menu... Nothing. Then stared back at the phone like I had to be missing something—the number menu usually showed which button to press. Then I saw it... The little message, barely noticeable on the bottom of the keypad, "For room service - see bottom right corner of menu."

Bottom right corner of the menu...

Shamefully and slowly I looked back at the menu. A QR code staring me right in the face.

No... I'd become one of those people... The people that needed the extra message... Why was it so damn small though! I didn't even notice it!

Here I was, about to call the front desk... Just to have someone tell me I needed to scan a damn code.

Letting out a sigh, I added my order, room number and name, "Order sent."

Great, twenty-five minute ETA. Onto research while I wait.

Madelyn Bennett. That was the name she'd given us. She was most likely from Washington and the thing she remembered the most was hiking and the smell of the outdoors. Maybe she was in a hiking accident?

Searched.

The top headline from one year ago...damn... *'Woman Found at The Bottom of a Cliff.'*

Instant click. This was it.

I barely had to scroll before I knew. This had to be Maddie.

Woman found at the bottom of a cliff, off a hiking trail in Washington. Hiking with her partner, who called in the accident, and she was airlifted to the hospital.

My eyes narrowed in on the screen. Was she walking off the path or did she fall from it? How'd her partner get far enough away that she fell off the cliff? The article didn't give many details, but I was side-eyeing him a bit on this one. I scrolled further.

In her partner's statement he claims he, "Wasn't paying attention for what felt like just a moment. Then he heard her scream. She must not have seen the drop, he told police."

Sure. A bit suspicious if you ask me, but ok. We weren't true crime detectives now too, I guess.

But now I knew she was most likely still at that hospital we talked about. Even scanning to the bottom, I didn't see anything about a transfer—even for longer-term care.

If Bridget can get that object, that's all we'd need. As long as she's still there.

I wondered if Maia was finding anything else—she might actually go a little more true crime on this than me. Watch her save a spirit and solve a crime. I wouldn't put it past her though. The thought did make me laugh though, 'But I said I wasn't paying attention!' Sure buddy.

I clicked the link, copied it and texted Maia.

"Hey, I think I found something here. This really sounds like it could be Maddie. What'd you think?"

I didn't even necessarily think she'd respond, if she was already sleeping, it was deserved.

Then my phone buzzed.

"THIS! I found the same one! I'm also doing a deeper dive. But I'm pretty sure it's Maddie too. I'll let you know if I find more."

"Geez, remember to get some sleep too! We still have some time remember."

"I will, I will, all good! Good night!"

Jesus, she's going to have a murder solved by morning.

I shook my head, put my phone on the nightstand, and closed out the article. Now I just needed to breathe for a minute. Tonight was a lot, these last few weeks had been a lot. But I also couldn't help but think about what was coming up.

Now I just wanted to let my thoughts spiral for a minute. Actually let myself think and wonder...What would it actually be like. Not for us, Maia, myself, or Bridget, but for them. We're helping these spirits that don't remember their lives and don't realize they're not even dead, they're just injured and trying to heal. We're kind of reintroducing them back to their own selves. Would I have questions if that happened to me? Would I be worried about taking the chance and going back? Are they possibly content enough being in The Crypt that any of them may turn down the offer we're giving them?

Maybe not even 'content' with The Crypt—that's not the right word. But they're content enough that it sounds better than the risk of the unknown. That's unnerving, even for them. They've become accustomed to The Crypt and the longer they're there, the more they forget the outside world... If I was in that position I might even think what's being told to me is a lie. Do they have the capacity to think that way? They've seen other spirits leave and never return maybe they'll think this is what happened?

Oh man, I was falling down the rabbit hole, but I hadn't thought of these things! This is what happens when I'm left alone with my thoughts. Nothing good normally comes from it.

But maybe I should be thinking about these things. It doesn't seem like anyone else is. Bridget seems so guilt-ridden she just wants them out. Maia just wants to help them. But what if something does happen during the process? What if they decline the reconnection? What could that do? They trust Bridget and she would be there, which was good, but we needed a real game plan, and a backup plan.

I really did need to talk to Bridget and Maia about this.

Snapping me out of my thoughts with a jolt, there was a knock on my door and a voice, "Room service! I'll just leave it at the door for you."

I gasped I was so excited, my stomach joining with a grumble. Oh, I could smell it through the door!

Cracking the door open, a low cart with a dinner tray left covered sat just outside. So fancy, my gosh!

Seeing they had left it for me and no one was waiting with it outside, I let the door fall open and rest on my foot. Did I pull the whole cart inside or just carry the tray?

Thankfully, hanging just slightly lower than the tray, an actually large card on the side, facing my door, read, *'Leave empty tray on cart when finished.'*

Asked and answered.

Shrugging and reaching to grab the full tray, I stopped. One more note caught my eye.

Folded neatly in the corner, next to the tray but propped like a nameplate. This one had my name on the front.

'Aly.'

But, something felt strange about this one. I didn't know why, but something in me did not like that note.

Why did this feel so weird? They probably do this for all their guests... Was that just too fancy? Could I just not handle that amount of posh? Come on now, Aly.

I had to be overthinking.

Still staring down at the note, all of this running through my head, I finally snatched it from the cart. Still hesitant, I slowly opened it to see.

Understanding sinking in.

This was not a simple nameplate.

Was this a sick joke? A prank?

I couldn't move. I could barely breathe. I was frozen, standing in the doorway... All I could do was stare at those words written in front of me, *'Found you. - Reaper.'*

Chapter 14

Standing there, my hands were shaking, still holding the note. The note he'd left me. He'd been here. He'd found me. He could be standing right in front of me but I couldn't even bring myself to look up.

The words were blurring together as I stared at them, *'Found you.'*

I had to make my feet move, make my hands function. I wanted to call out to Bridget but my brain couldn't even think properly. I also didn't want to mess up anything she was in the middle of.

Maybe he knew that. Maia was safe at home, Bridget wasn't here, the perfect opportunity for him.

Finally, my fingers released the delicately folded card, letting it fall to the floor. My name now facing up at me, written on the top. Taunting me.

He was here—or had been here. I could practically feel the chill of his breath on my neck. Every inch of me was panicking the longer I stood in this doorway.

At last, my arms found movement, pushing through the panic to reach for the tray. I needed to get back inside the room. I needed the barrier of the door closed behind me. I didn't dare steal a glance in front of the cart or down the hall. I couldn't risk losing a single moment of focus.

Lifting the tray, my feet carried me back like they suddenly had a mind of their own. One that matched my desperation and had been waiting for me to just grab the food to go.

Shoving the door shut behind me, I quickly placed the food on the bed. The tray was stable enough and my knees were already buckling under me. I couldn't keep myself up. I'd gotten back in, the door was shut, the food was here, and at this point I didn't even care if it got a little cold. He couldn't get in here. I let myself collapse to the floor, hugging my knees to my chest.

I didn't even take the flashlight, I hadn't even touched it, and he still found me... How?

Because of the dream? Going into the Crypt again? We were safe in our homes, but maybe our minds weren't safe as soon as we were back in his world... Could he have been in the Crypt the whole time and we just didn't know—until he wanted us to?

I was shaking my head in disbelief. How powerful was he?

Bridget said I was underestimating Maia... I think we were all underestimating someone else...

I cursed under my breath. What was going on? How were we supposed to do anything with him breathing down our necks like this? Feeling like he was lurking around any corner—hiding within any shadow.

Still on the floor, my head in my hands, I felt like I could cry. This was supposed to be a relaxing night away but instead I'm being haunted and taunted! Could I even sleep without him invading my dreams?

This turmoil was killing me. I needed to breathe. Slow... In, out, I was trying to remind myself. In—out. I had to breathe. Get it together.

Everything had been building up and this final straw just blew the lid right off and sent me spinning.

Finally, my breath began steadying, my mind started to clear and pulling my head from my hands, I knew I must be a mess, but I didn't care. I was alone. I stopped because I realized, this was exactly what he wanted. He wanted me going crazy. He wanted me breaking down and feeling watched. He didn't want me to feel safe. How would that help him?

No. He wanted me to feel like I couldn't win against him. Like there was nothing I could do so why even try. He wanted me to feel weak. That was his first mistake.

He wasn't going to make me break. I wasn't going to let him make me vulnerable. Whatever he was trying to pull right now, it wasn't going to work. This time, he fumbled.

Slowly, I pulled myself off the floor. I didn't even care how I looked, I didn't care to go clean myself up in the bathroom first, my food was here and I was hungry. He wasn't ruining that too.

God, I needed that burger right now.

Then, yet again, I was stopped, jolted by a crash on the back window.

"Dammit!" The note was one thing, but a physical sound now? "Come on! I'm just trying to have a freaking meal!" But of course, I had to see what the hell that was.

With a groan, I stalked over to the balcony window. No way was I going outside, but I could see if I saw anything from the door.

Nothing looked out of place right away—the table and chairs hadn't moved, the table was still set with the small unlit lantern candle, nothing new, nothing moved. Then I saw it. A small, smooth pebble on the floor of the balcony. Did something throw a stone at my window? I'm on the second floor...

My eyes narrowed to scan the dark grounds below the balcony. How could anything other than a bird reach this far? There were some trees not far from my room, maybe it was a bird? I couldn't see anything from this angle.

A loud caw sounded across the sky, as if my thoughts summoned it. A crow?

I couldn't see anything above the trees the sky was way too dark at this point. This place barely lit up the grass out the back here. But I could hear it. One final caw, lower, drawing my eyes back to the ground. There he was. The hooded dark figure, standing at the edge of the woods.

He couldn't get inside the room, he couldn't get to me here. But he was watching, waiting.

He made no motion for me to come outside. It seemed like he couldn't speak into my mind while I was still inside, so he just stood there a moment. Did he just want me to be curious? Intrigued? I knew what his overall goal was, but I definitely didn't understand all these games...

I needed to reach out to Bridget, but in a non-urgent way. Not to interrupt her. Hopefully she would be finished with her part of the plan tonight.

For now, I just waited. I wasn't moving. I stood with my arms crossed, staring him down. I was over it. I wanted to eat. He wanted a reaction that he wasn't going to get.

Instead, I gave my own bird signal with a single finger and closed the blinds.

Cursing, stomping away from the balcony, "Bullshit Reaper, making my burger get cold." I could signal to Bridget once I was full."

"So... Uh... Nothing urgent, but whenever you're done in there, could you pop back over here please?" I sent out the signal to Bridget down the bond. I really didn't want to rush her, but I did need to talk to her.

"What's wrong?"

"Nothing's wrong. Everything's fine, just trying to keep you in the loop." But I knew she could sense it.

"You're being too nice."

Well ok, that was a little dramatic.

"Hey! I'm always nice. If it was urgent I would say so."

"But it can't wait until morning?"

"Why are you being difficult?"

"Why are you?"

Oh my God, Bridget.

"Just get the item, then come talk to me! Is that so difficult?"

"Fine."

Jeez, these witches sometimes, so pushy!

"Alright, I'm here." It had only been about twenty minutes.

"See that was quick. There was no need to rush through. You didn't rush did you? You finished what you needed to?"

"I didn't rush. I got what I needed. I was just about to have it when you called out."

"And you were about to ruin it all when I said come when you're done." I wagged my finger and shook my head in disapproval, "Come on now. Tsk, tsk."

"Well, I got it done and I'm here now. So what happened?"

"Yes... Ok... So anyway. Umm... The Reaper was here—is here."

"He's here?" Bridget said it loud enough that if she were alive the next room probably would've heard, "He found you here?"

"Yes. Apparently not taking the light didn't matter since we went into The Crypt. Seems like he can't get in the room, at least not if he's already tried, but he left a note with my dinner. It had my name on it... Then he was standing outside near my balcony—he wanted my attention. He wanted to scare me."

"A scared mind is a weak mind." Bridget's arms were crossed but her narrowed eyes widened with understanding. "You can't let him get to you, Aly."

"I know. Maia needs to know too." But I still had pause. "I understand what he's doing, I just don't understand how it helps him. Does he think he's just intimidating enough or does something about us being scared help him trap us?"

"I wish I had a true answer to that... But I think it's mind games and power plays. He doesn't want you to feel confident taking him on. It might just be that he thinks if you're scared enough you won't stop him. Or, if you're confidence is dampened you won't have the strength to... It could also just be a power play."

"So basically, there could be a reason or he's just trying to talk shit in a weird way."

Bridget laughed but nodded and shrugged, "Yes, I guess that's also a way to put it."

She suddenly looked down and sighed. She had a sort of reminiscent look in her eye, "Gosh Madam Selene would have loved you and Maia. It's a shame you two were so far down the line of descendants."

"We're going to help them too, Bridget. Not just the human souls. Everyone."

She returned a sad smile. She was truly haunted by that place and she still had to live in it. Still haunted by the memories that trapped her there.

"Did you learn what you needed? About Maddie? Any new helpful leads to help with item track?"

"I think so. I sent Maia an article too but I haven't heard more from her. She's either gone down the rabbit hole herself or she's asleep now."

"Well, you should also try to be doing that. The getting some sleep part."

"I know." I couldn't help but glance at the window. "I've been putting it off, but I'm exhausted."

"He can't come in here. He also can't get into your actual dreams. Just so you know. It doesn't work like that."

"No?" I whipped my head at her.

"Nope. You're safe." She sauntered over to the couch that sat just next to the bed, "But if you'd like, I can stay with you, just in case."

I believed her when she said it, but seeing her sit down like that... Now I actually felt it. The safety. I wasn't alone.

"You don't sleep?"

"Girl, I'm a ghost."

I laughed, "My bad. I've never seen it I wasn't sure."

"Shut your eyes and relax. I can see the moon out the window—that's plenty relaxing for me."

I woke up to the sun blazing through the window. Bright enough that I could already feel the warmth on my face from across the room.

Peeking one eye open, the light stung first waking up. Bridget was still laid out on the couch, her eyes closed—if

I didn't know any better, I'd have thought she was trying to sunbathe.

I knew she wasn't sleeping—she didn't, she couldn't, that had been confirmed last night.

I wondered if this was the first night she'd actually stayed outside The Crypt. I hadn't thought about it before, but she hadn't really talked about it either. I didn't even know what kind of space she'd set up for herself—the type of home she'd put together. I would never judge her for it. But maybe she didn't want to share, maybe it was just the timing whenever we had been in there. Right now it didn't matter though, I'd never seen her more at peace.

Instead of disturbing her peaceful image, I checked my phone for the time and any messages from Maia.

Only 6:00AM and no notifications, no text, no call. Looks like everyone was enjoying the quiet of the morning. I know I didn't want to move yet.

Everything had been moving so quickly lately we hadn't had a moment like this in days. A moment to actually feel normal, stretch out on the bed, under the warm morning sun, and get ready for a slow morning. Made me kind of wish for a witchy moment where coffee and breakfast could suddenly start floating to me just because I thought about it. Mmm, that would just be the cherry on top.

I stole another glance at Bridget, hoping she wouldn't notice. Wouldn't feel me staring. Could she feel the warmth or just see the light through her eyelids? I had so

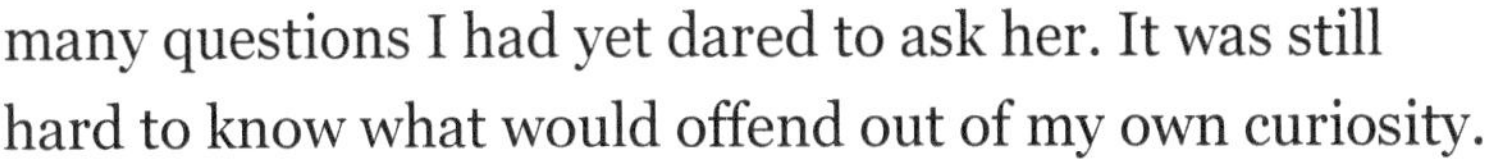

many questions I had yet dared to ask her. It was still hard to know what would offend out of my own curiosity.

"You just going to keep staring or did you have something to say?"

Shoot.

"Oh, uh—sorry. I wasn't trying to stare. I didn't realize…" I couldn't find the words, I wasn't expecting a response.

"I've been in The Crypt a long time, Aly. Remember? I can sense when I'm being watched."

Right. The Reaper. She'd had to really train and hone her senses to know exactly when and where he'd be showing up. It was survival. Of course she'd have felt it. Now I felt stupid.

"I'm sorry. I didn't have a question. I was just thinking how peaceful you looked… I've never seen you like that."

She paused, letting the words sink in. She opened her eyes to look at me then.

"The Crypt has always been a dark place. Now that I've been coming out, it's still always been nighttime. You were still sleeping and I realized this was the first time I've been out in the sun in a long time… Even if we are technically inside still. I was just trying to remember how it felt."

Tears actually welled in my eyes. God, I wish breaking this curse with The Crypt could give her a second chance. Not just keep her around for Maia and I, but a real life.

"Can you feel anything? Like in The Crypt, do you feel cold? Or when we're within the bond together with Maia, can you feel our touch?"

"Physical touch like that, yes. But only within the bond. I can feel you two. But in The Crypt, no. I don't get the same chills you might feel."

"Huh." Sad, but interesting. It did give me an idea for later though.

"Have you heard from Maia yet?" Bridget was clearly ready to change the subject. I didn't blame her.

"Uh, not yet. But it's after 9AM for her, so it shouldn't be long." I confirmed, checking my phone once more.

"When do you need to get home?"

"Check out is 11. I set Wes up to feed the dog this morning so I'll be ok a few more hours... Why? Are you wanting to start the connection this morning?" I knew we wanted to do it soon, as soon as possible, I guess I just didn't think that would be now.

"I have a plan. I think we should try. The sooner we know this will work, the better. Then I can fill you both in."

I narrowed my eyes at her. It was too early for this cryptic shit.

"Ugh. What now? What plan?"

"No, no, Aly. I think you're actually going to like this one. I know Maia will. But I don't want to get either of your hopes up, so I want to make sure this will work first."

"Oh, well Maia definitely liking it for sure isn't selling it."

"Oh hush. Just relax for once. Like me." She said with a grin. "And text Maia. She taking too long. Let's see if she's up—see what she's figured out."

⚜

Maia was three hours ahead so it was late enough that I wouldn't be waking her. A call would be easier and faster.

"Oh, I've learned so much!"

No hi, hello, good morning. It sounded like she hadn't even slept—just completely consumed with research.

"Well good morning detective." I laughed and put the phone on speaker.

"Yes, sorry, hi, hello, good morning! Ooh, you know, now I don't know if I like detective or Madam better."

"Madam detective?" Bridget chimed in.

"Oh, that's more like it. I can switch around."

"Anyways… Are you going to tell us or just keep coming up with a name?"

"My bad. Jeez. Have some coffee and let me have my fun." I could hear her flipping pages in the background, she'd been taking notes. "Ok. First off—pretty sure I not only know where Maddie is but also figured out what

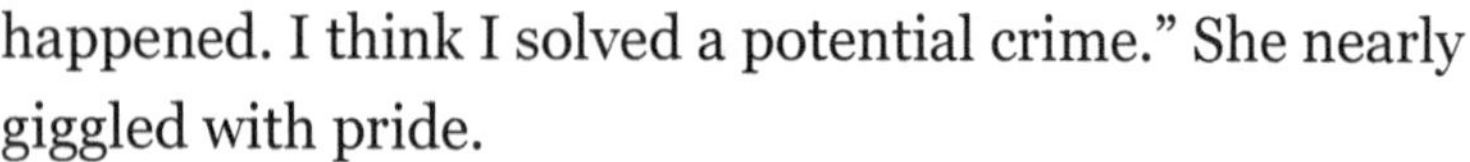

happened. I think I solved a potential crime." She nearly giggled with pride.

Called it.

"How did I know that was the kind of rabbit hole you'd end up going down?"

"How could I not? Especially with the article you sent me. Her partner was hiking with her and just so happened to not be paying attention at the right moment? It only took minutes for her to fall over the edge? Come on now—I think not."

"Ok. So… How about we save the Nancy Drew investigations for after? Don't get me wrong, I'm here for it. Let's just save her first?"

Bridget mouthed 'Thank you.' I just nodded and smirked.

"Yes, yes, you're right. Sorry. There's just so much! I got excited. You know how excited I get about these things." More shuffling. "Not related to the unsolved mystery, she's definitely still at that hospital. From what it sounds like, they had to put her in a coma due to injuries. However, the scary thing we all know, is when they do that, there is the potential of not waking up."

I glanced sideways at Bridget, wondering if Maia would say what I was thinking next.

"Has she been in a coma the whole time? The full year?"

"It looks like it. I think… I think we're her solution to waking up."

She said it.

"That's why she hasn't come out yet—she's disconnected."

"Exactly. I think that's what's going on here. Maybe not at first... But for some reason I feel like her soul was hanging around, waiting, and then wandered off. Then she ended up in The Crypt and obviously, couldn't reconnect."

"That actually makes sense."

Bridget was sitting up now, "Maia, would you be ready to try making the connection this morning?"

"Like now?" She was as surprised as I had been.

"I know it's a little sudden, but we've gotten the info we need and I did get your anchor item."

"Oh... Ok."

"I know, Maia. It sounds a little crazy to do it right away." I jumped in. "But Bridget seems to have a plan up her sleeve if this goes well. She hasn't even filled me in yet but supposedly, we're both going to like it. Especially you. Her words."

Silence filled the room for a moment. Waiting for Maia's response.

"Interesting."

My eyes shifted from Maia to Bridget. "Is that a yes?"

"Can we know the plan now? Since I'm here?"

"Once this first one is done." Bridget's voice was firm, not mean, but she was not kidding. This tone was not to be pushed.

"Fine. Can I prepare first?"

"Prepare? What?"

"Aly, some of us need to mentally prepare for these things. I'd also like to grab my crystals, a candle, and some herbs real quick if that's ok."

"Jeez, I didn't know what you meant." Snarky, snarky.

"I'll call you back in a few."

Maia hung up and Bridget looked at me.

"You should prepare yourself as well. I'm going into the space now to get ready for you both." She stood from the couch, straightening her clothes, "When you have Maia back, call down the bond and I'll bring you both in."

Just before she vanished again, I held up a hand, "Wait! I meant to ask you before. I've been thinking and I'm a little worried about just one outcome."

She tilted her head, concern written on her face. "What's that?"

"We're going to be doing this with a lot of spirits, and they may not all have the same reaction. I don't think Maddie would do this but you never truly know... What if the help is refused? Like they don't believe us or they're just too afraid to take the chance of leaving The Crypt."

To my surprise, I saw her body tense, taken aback by the question. Like she hadn't thought about that either.

Like she was biting through the tension, she sighed. "Sadly, we can't always save everyone. As much as I want to. I believe that at least most, if not all, the spirits will accept the help. But all we can do is try."

We sat there, in a moment of silence together. How could I respond? I wanted an answer that gave a solution, a course of action… I wanted an answer that told me even if they started with a no, we could make it a yes. But it just wasn't that simple.

So I nodded, "All we can do is try."

"I know that may not be what you want to hear. That's not what I want to say. But it's the sad truth—the reality. We might not be able to save them all. But we can most certainly try."

Then she was gone.

Chapter 15

This was it. We were about to make our first connection, form our first bridge. Maia's idea for mental preparation wasn't sounding so crazy anymore.

Looking over towards the balcony, the sun still pouring through the window, between the curtains. I normally would've closed them by now, but for some reason I hadn't touched them since arriving last night.

The night sky had been calming and this natural warmth felt good. But right now it was just a little too much. Focus required darkness and there was no more time to procrastinate.

But just as quickly as I could push myself off the bed, another idea stopped me.

Looking at the curtain, then down at my hand—if I can light a candle... Could I move a curtain? That shouldn't be that hard—that different. I mean, I created a flame with my mind, what's moving a little curtain?

I moved slightly closer, away from the bed and any potential barriers.

I really didn't understand how all of this worked still. I just knew my attention needed to be on the curtains and what I wanted them to do.

Standing at the end of the bed, I closed my eyes and started picturing it. Narrowing my thoughts in on the curtains, like nothing else existed in the room. I could see them begin to sway, begin to close over the door. I pictured them moving closer together, shutting all the remaining sunlight out of the room—the rings gliding along the top bar, not harshly, but in one smooth swift movement. The same image as if an invisible figure were closing them in front of me.

I let that scene play on loop in my head, not once, not twice, but over and over to keep my focus. Like my mind was now specifically trying to communicate with the curtain itself.

Slow and steady, I raised my hand, letting it curve—my fingers guiding the motion to pull the curtain to the opposing wall. It was like giving them a light nudge from a distance. And they listened.

It didn't rush closed, but there was no restraint, it just listened. Not even a verbal cue.

I did it.

All I could do was stand there, blinking, baffled. Staring at my hand again and back at the curtain.

Finally, a laugh burst out of me, "What the hell?"

I wondered if any other witches had similar reactions back in Salem when they started discovering what they could do.

Were they excited too? Did they think they were going insane? Laugh in shock? Were they scared of themselves?

How had I never figured any of this out before? I mean, obviously, I'm not trying to move things with my mind everyday but what little kid hasn't tried to get the remote to come into their hand without moving?

None of this started until Bridget told us what we were… Was it something that really did need to be activated or something?

Bridget had said something, sort of like that. She said there were things that wouldn't work properly if we didn't want to believe or already believe… Was that it? Anything before had been a silly game out of laziness and now I wanted to see what I was really capable of so it triggered it?

How was it that simple to unleash? This other world inside my world was wild.

What else could I try?

My eyes were already darting, scanning the room to then quickly fall on the giant bath and faucet in the corner of the room. That!

Buzzzzz... Buzzzzzz... Dammit! Like freaking clockwork. Snapping me back. Maia was calling.

I looked back at the tub, "I'll be back for you later." *Buzzzzz... Buzzzzzz...* "Alright, alright."

"Hey Maia. Ready?"

"All good. I'm nice and zen now. Did you prepare?"

"Uhh, you could say that... I learned I can also move things with my mind. I closed my curtains to focus better."

Silence. Maia's response was simply silence.

"You there?"

"You prepared to make our very first connection, to create our very first spirit bridge, by closing the curtains with your mind? You *can* close the curtains with your mind?" Maia's tone over each word was a bit judgy if you ask me.

"You have your way, I have mine. I thought you'd at least be a little more interested but I'll give the judgy tone a pass." I waved my hand, swatting her tone like she could see me. "Anyway, I've got you on speaker. Bridget is already waiting down the bond. I'm going to let her know we're ready."

In a few moments, Bridget would be pulling us back to our space. The three of us, deep within the bond, our minds locked together. This was it. Time to steal our first soul back from The Reaper.

It was hard to forget what it felt like inside the bond. It sounds like it would be a happy, pleasant place... Not that it was dark and scary, but it wasn't exactly sunshine and rainbows. I wasn't sure where it would be located—maybe the back of our minds, similar to whenever people say they hear that voice in that back of their head, or when you get that creeping feeling of intuition. This was different though. I couldn't quite put my finger on why, but it felt more like we were near the front. Like we were just beyond the front doors to all of us and we were just waiting to be let in.

The strangest part, oddly enough, was being pulled in. Going into The Crypt felt like letting sleep take over and finding yourself in the most vivid dream you've ever experienced. It never felt like reality, even though it still was.

Being pulled into the bond was being pulled into a dark, shapeless, limitless space. It was more like you were in some spiritual waiting room rather than just simply your own mind. And once I was there, even though darkness fully surrounded me, I was the only thing staying still. There was movement all around me.

Was I feeling my thoughts racing? Wouldn't that be funny.

Then I realized, it wasn't me moving or my thoughts racing. It was the bond connection forming. Bridget had never pulled us into our own minds where we could then see each other—she pulled us in and then pulled us together. We were three becoming one through the bond.

Suddenly, the rushed movement stopped. Adjusting to two slower, figured movements. Their shapes forming as Bridget and Maia came into view.

Now I was understanding all my feelings from the first time. Nothing had made sense before. But, I was finally paying attention and part of me hated that I was kind of starting to love it.

I gave a slow sigh as we joined together in our formation, Bridget and Maia now fully visible.

"Hello girls." Bridget had fully appeared now. "Are we ready to begin?"

I looked from Bridget to Maia. Maia had appeared just before Bridget, now on my right. The only light was a pale glow in the middle of the three of us. It looked like Bridget might be holding it... Had she conjured it? I had thought it was the energy we brought together.

Maybe I was wrong.

"Maia, here is your anchor." Bridget handed her a light scarf. "Maddie has been wearing it since the day she arrived in The Crypt. She's always said that though she doesn't remember much, somehow that scarf helps her still feel alive. I have a good feeling about this one." She gave me a knowing look, "She wants to fight."

"If she wears it everyday, how were you able to get it?" Maia was moving it around in her hands, getting a feel for it.

"I told her that you two had an idea that could help her in this new life. It could help bring back her memories and maybe even more. She was more than happy to hand it over."

"Does she know what you are?" My expression inquisitive. Bridget simply nodded in response.

I looked at Maia then and Bridget quickly clarified, "But not you two. I trust her, but still, for your safety, she only knows about me."

I let out a tight breath. "So Maia just needs to focus on the scarf and let it guide her to wherever Maddie's body is?"

"Precisely. Focus in, but leave your mind open. Once you've found her, Aly, you will slip into her mind with her. I will go get Maddie. I've already told her where to be. On my signal, you'll open the portal."

"The portal is the bridge?"

"It's half of it. Once Maddie's through the portal we'll see if she can merge on her own. All she needs to do is make contact with the body."

"And if she can't?" Did she mean this might not work?

"If she can't, you bridge the gap."

"I just grab both her hand and her human hand?" That sounded weird as hell to say.

"If needed." Bridget was a little too nonchalant on that last part.

"Alright, let's..."

"Wait."

Bridget was reaching for both our hands but paused as Maia cut her off.

"What happens after the connections? Are we just pulled back here? Do we pull ourselves back? You're always the one putting us places, I don't want to be just standing there..." She had a point. And Maia never cut Bridget off.

"I'm sorry for the rush." But she didn't move her hands. "Once the connection is made, I'll pull you both back. Just signal down the bond and say, 'It's done.'"

For a moment, I was a little surprised, taken aback really.

"Bridget... I know we're testing things on this first one, but Maddie has been your friend... Do you not want to come with us to see it complete? Before we leave her?"

"For now, I have said my good-byes to Maddie. I've been in The Crypt long enough to have had many good-bye's, unfortunately. This is the first good one." She spoke like she was fine, but I could see tears wetting her eyes. "My hope is that with this plan, if I can stay around, and she's around you, Aly, I can maybe pay her another visit in the future. Maybe I can pay more lost souls a visit once they're found. Some still remember their lives or parts of it, so maybe they'll also remember this. Time will tell. For now, I've already had to make peace. But thank you, I appreciate the sentiment."

Maia and I had taken her hands now and she gave us both a squeeze.

"Alright. Now are we ready?"

Maia held up the scarf with one hand, gripping into it tighter, and closed her eyes for focus.

"Ready."

The three of us stood there, joining hands, fully connected, Bridget and I fully focused on Maia. This bond connection was so strange but continued to fascinate me.

I felt her mind tracking. I couldn't see where she was going but I could feel the rush of the movements. The paths her mind was flowing through. It was sending pins and needles through my fingers, down my arms, and all the way to the back of my neck.

"Tell us when you see anything significant." Bridget was quick with her comment, not meaning to distract.

"I thought I would start in my own room—where we got started here tonight. But I started on the cliff, where

Maddie was found. I think I started where her trauma began."

I glanced at Bridget quickly. I don't think she could tell what I was thinking. Probably best for now.

We had Maddie's scarf... If we weren't just tracking her body... If we could actually access memories through the objects could we find other memories too? If we had something else would it be possible to track memories farther back?

Maia's detective mind would love where my thought process was going.

"I traveled with her. A lot was going on. She was a bit in and out which isn't surprising." Maia continued her narration. "I saw the sign she was talking about. She's in the hospital."

We were almost there.

"Ok. I pulled myself out. I wasn't sure what my point of view was. But I couldn't see where she was. We're in the hospital room now. The doctor is talking. I think to her parents. They are talking about how Maddie was placed in a coma. The hope is that she'll wake up and continue healing, but she said there's of course no guarantee."

So we were right on that.

"Ok, you're seeing the memories from the scarf, can you see if she's still there? Can you see present day?"

Her face scrunched as she focused. "Yes, she's still there. Her parents aren't there right now. She's getting the regular nurse check-in."

"Are you doing ok, Maia?"

"I'm fine." Her eyes were still closed. "She wanted me to see those memories."

"She wanted you to see them?"

"The scarf warmed up as soon as I was being guided through that part, like it was telling me I needed to wait. Once I was ok, it went cold."

Was Maddie's subconscious afraid of something being forgotten? Enough that a piece of trauma clung to the scarf to be found?

I kept wanting to say I'd never heard of these things before, but I haven't heard of any of this before!

In that moment, I looked at Bridget. "Something still inside of her wanted us to know what happened. Something needed us to know. She got hurt but I really don't think it was her fault."

We paused, both of us thinking. The trauma, the fall, the hiking, the man, her own memories—alive and while in The Crypt... Her memories... Her memory! "We don't know what she'll remember when she wakes up. We don't know if that guy is still around... This could be why it was held on so tight."

Maia gasped, "What if—"

"When she wakes up, we need to get her away from him."

"What are you talking about? What do you mean? How are we supposed to do that?" Bridget was a ball of confusion, looking at me like I'd lost my mind. I mean, maybe I had, but that would've been partially on her.

"I don't know how yet, but we'll figure it out."

Bridget gave me a pressing look.

"Bridget, that man might have tried to kill her. If she can't remember anything when she wakes up and he's still around, why would she leave him? When all she knows is that he's the one that called for help?"

"Oh goodness... And he could try again?"

"Who knows, but we don't want to find out."

"Maia, is there anyone else there with her?"

"Not right now. I'm alone in the room with her now."

"Ok, are you ready for me to go get her?"

It was a long moment's pause before Maia let out a breath, "Yes. Aly, you coming?"

With a nod, Bridget squeezed my hand and mouthed, *You can do this.*

We both closed our eyes—not letting our hands go.

I needed to be able to do this. Maia was holding the space, Bridget was retrieving Maddie, I was the bridge.

All my senses needed to shift—channel into Maia's mind.

I focused on the initial rush that brought her to that room — the tingles sent down my arms, the sensations of the bond. I was already with her. I just needed to push.

I focused harder on the bond. The connection. I could do this. I had to.

Maybe it was like what I had tried before, with the candle and the curtain. With those I focused on what I wanted to happen, what I wanted them to do but I had to push out the energy, thrust it towards what I wanted… The connection was there, I felt everything Maia was feeling, I knew what I wanted, now I needed to push. Push my mind into hers. My energy into hers. Blend the pictures together…

I squeezed her hand, feeling my face scrunch and pushed all my energy towards her.

"You did it!"

I was looking right at Maia now, inside the hospital room. Maddie's body was in the bed. It worked!

Maia smiled and motioned to Maddie's body. "You made it to the party."

I crossed my arms, still looking at Maddie, "This is wild. And now we wait for Bridget's signal—are you ready?"

"The real question is, are you ready? You're the bridge."

"I have to be. But yes. Look at everything we've done so far."

"It has been wild. So much has changed and it's only been a couple of weeks."

So much had changed. Our whole worlds had flipped. This wasn't a job change, a move, or just life happening.

Two weeks ago life was normal. Now we were witches who communicated with the dead...what a sentence that was.

"I am still trying to understand though. I don't even know what to take from the memories that scarf was showing me." She finally looked at me then. "I thought I would be following it like some guiding light. But the closer we got the more it showed me. Like it was giving me a message."

"I know."

"We can't just leave her here. Once she's reconnected."

"I know."

This wasn't going according to plan. But Bridget cared about these lost souls. How could we not actually help the first one and fully save her life if we could? What would be the point of reconnecting her soul if it could just be torn from her yet again?...

"So what do we do? Bridget will be here any minute."

"I think all we can do to start..." I knew this might panic Bridget, but we had to know, "After we make the connection, let's see if she wakes up. Let's see if she remembers anything."

"Aly, open the portal, we're ready!" Bridget's voice came barreling down the bond.

I grabbed Maia's hand for support and turned my focus to the corner of the hospital room. They'd need some room to get in.

Opening the portal... I had to get this one right.

Bridget had briefly explained it but she couldn't demonstrate it. That was one of her restraints from The Crypt.

'Imagine The Crypt and think of the portal like an open window you're using to peek through. You need to think of The Crypt like you want to go there.' That's what she'd told me. Imagine The Crypt and then give it an open window.

So that's what I did.

I fully embraced it. Let my mind dive in like I could send myself there if I really wanted to.

I embraced the darkness it brought to my mind, the darkness of the trees and the energy. I pictured the trees surrounding me, the open field just beyond the bush we'd peek through, the roaming spirits, the rolling fog that covered the ground more and more the deeper you went. I even thought of the unknown creature that could be lurking in any hiding place you may encounter. I pictured it all. Like I was there.

I imagined Bridget and Maddie at that spot, just beyond the edge of the field, just out of sight of any wandering eyes. Then, I placed a window. I didn't picture the window though. I was asking for one. Asking my magic to place something for me to see into The Crypt.

Then, the glowing ball appeared. Growing, expanding, widening into the window I'd asked for. I could see Maddie and Bridget coming into view, Maddie's expression was pure shock. Bridget had a prideful smile.

One single wave of my hand was the last move and all it took. My portal was open.

Even I was in shock.

I'd lit the candle and moved the curtain... This was a damn portal! I did that! And it was staying—under my control.

I returned Bridget's smile, beckoning them to come through.

We were ready.

"I don't need the portal, I'll be watching from the bond." Bridget didn't speak but rather sent this message down the bond.

She also probably needed to keep watch.

"Maia can help her get through while I keep this open." I couldn't chance losing focus, not without more practice.

Thankfully, Maia heard her name and rushed over to take Maddie's hand. Ready for her first step over the threshold.

Maddie was more than ready—about ready to dive through as soon as I was signaling to come. I thought she may not have even needed the help until I felt it. Reaching through to take Maia's hand, I felt the pull. Like an extension of myself, the gentle force tugged on me. I felt it tug on Maddie too. But Maia's grip stayed strong, tightened.

Maddie wasn't expecting it but Maia's instincts kicked in and she pulled. The energy pushed back slightly, only from the friction, but Maia pulled against, pulling Maddie all the way through.

Maddie let out a breath, getting her footing. "Huh, wow. That was somethin'!" She let out a nervous giggle, looking around the room. "Wow, so this is what happened..."

This whole time, thinking she was dead... I'm not sure which is worse—thinking you're dead and stuck, or seeing your body in front of you still dying and hoping you can save yourself...

It felt a bit intrusive to just be standing here watching and waiting for her reaction... I wished we could give her a moment alone, but we were on a bit of a time crunch. This should all be fixed soon anyway.

"Bridget told me a little of what was going on, but I don't know what I was expecting..."

Fully understood where she was coming from there. That had been my life these last couple of weeks.

"I thought I was dead in this world—am I?"

Before responding I made another wave with my hand and closed the portal. We couldn't keep it open for any potential strays and I wasn't going to be able to bridge anything if I was focused on that.

"No, you're not dead. That's actually why you're here. Your soul ended up in that place because your body has been struggling to heal. That place is more of a limbo…"

I looked at the body in the hospital bed.

"Bridget told you we could help you regain your memories and possibly more right?"

"Yes, that's what she said. Is that really possible?" Her eyes widened as if she just noticed her own self in the bed. "Is that me? My body trying to heal?"

"That is, but don't worry. What we need to do is really easy, super simple." I walked closer to be next to her on the bed. "All those memories should come back to you. You just have to reconnect with yourself. Come and hold your hand."

Maddie's eyes lit up, I thought I was even seeing some tears coming, "Are you saying I could even be alive again?" Her excitement didn't last long though, "Will I still have these new memories, though? Will I be able to see you two? Will I remember Bridget?"

The questions. She had to ask the questions I was worried about. The ones with answers I was worried would change her mind.

Biting my lip, I took her hand, "Maddie, I wish I could say yes for sure—but we don't know yet. All I can say, is that not reconnecting is the worse option."

"What happens if I don't?"

There was no point in sugar coating it. She needed to make this connection or she'd turn into another Reaped spirit. I couldn't let him have a single win. Not even one. I felt like, especially in this case, the best option was to just tell the truth.

"Maddie, if you don't reconnect, you will die."

Even Maia was shocked by my blunt reaction. But it needed to be said.

"There is a spirit, a negative energy, who is harvesting souls from that limbo. We're trying to keep you from being next. I know you want to remember. We want you to remember us too. But we can cross that bridge when we get there."

Maddie looked from me to herself in the bed. "Ok. I'll trust you. Bridget trusts you. She's pretty much trusted you with her life." I felt her guard dropping, her mind embracing me as she walked to join me next to the bed. "I just take her—my hand?"

I was the bridge, her soul knew it, her mind knew it. The dots were connecting. The tension was releasing as she was allowing me in. I don't think she even realized it, she just needed to trust. That was the key.

"That's it. That simple."

Before making the move, she looked down a final moment at herself. I didn't blame any nerves. If I were in her shoes, I'd be nervous too. Get my hopes up, then what if it didn't work. What if it did but you'd already forgotten so much that it was like you didn't know that person anymore? The one you once were. You didn't know that life or if you even liked it before. Would you know you wanted it back for sure? The only reason to take the chance was because you knew death was closer in your current state now. Maddie wasn't dead yet, but was closer now if she didn't take the chance.

I could see the nerves in her eyes, but also the sympathy. Like she was looking at someone else entirely.

Her moment didn't last long. Just a moment for herself before her delicate, ghost hand reached out for her body, stretching for her hand.

She didn't have to say anything for it to work, but I don't think those three little whispered words were meant for that. I think they were just meant for her, just before making contact. Those three little whispered words.

"Take me home."

Chapter 16

Time stood still. I would've believed you if you had told me the whole world was frozen. Waiting. I would've even believed we'd caused it. Maia and I both standing still as boards, holding our breath, afraid to even move an inch. Watching.

Seeing Maddie's hand reach out to connect with her sleeping one was so painfully slow. It was like watching a fairy tale, waiting to see if true love's kiss would work. Well, maybe if this was a Grimm's fairy tale…

No one made a sound, not even Bridget, who was now silently watching from down the bond.

This was the moment we'd all been waiting for. Our first connection. Would Maddie slowly fade away or quickly vanish? Would it work at all? Everything had gone as planned so far, so perfectly. So perfect, it was almost too perfect.

I couldn't breathe seeing Maddie make contact, every muscle in my body tense as her fingers slipped over the top of her hand. Then it started. Her soul knew—knew it was home and it was more than ready to latch on.

Slowly, she crept her fingers further into that sleeping grip, working to fully lock hold. But as her grasp closed in deeper, the more she disappeared.

This was the first time since seeing The Crypt that I'd been happy to see any ghost disappearing. It was working! It was really working. Our first step towards victory. Our first test passing. My eyes burned as I blinked away a single tear.

I took Maia's hand, we'd both been standing, staring, watching in silence.

"Maia. We can actually do this." That's what this truly meant. Helping Maddie was one amazing thing, but this was so much more.

She turned to me then, her eyes also gleaming, "We can."

Bridget's voice came down the bond, "Girls?"

"It's done, Bridget. She reconnected."

We all gave another moment of silence before I remembered, Bridget was about to pull us back.

"Wait! Bridget!" I nearly yelled it, it just blurted out so quickly. "Don't pull us back yet."

"What? Why? Aly, The Reaper is tracking you—what are you doing?" Her tone a bit accusing. She knew we were hiding something.

"We need her to wake up first." I looked at Maia to double check that she was still with me on this one. She, of course, closed her eyes and nodded in return.

"Aly—no, it's too risky." Bridget was bewildered. "She may not wake up anytime soon..."

"You want to save these souls right?"

Bridget's silence was deafening.

"And you did."

"Bridget, someone tried to kill her. We don't know what she'll remember—from being alive or from The Crypt. What if he's still out there? We can't just let it happen again."

"And if she doesn't know who you two are?"

"Well, that's where we start... We're kind of winging this here! But do you want to help her or not? What's the bigger risk? Walking away or staying?" We both knew the answer.

"Oh, we should not be doing this." Bridget muttered. "Fine. But I'm watching. One bad sign and I'm yanking you both out."

"Deal."

"Oh, I swear, if I could get headaches you both would be a constant." With that Bridget went quiet. She was always so dramatic, jeez.

"So... What now?" Maia looked from me to Maddie.

"I guess—now we wait. See if she will wake up."

"This is agonizing! How long is this supposed to take?" Maia was slumped against the hospital room chair as we waited for Maddie to hopefully wake up.

"I'm a witch, not a psychic. And it's only been ten minutes Maia, chill." She still rolled her eyes at me.

"Is there anything we can do?"

"I think if anyone knew how to wake a coma patient a lot more people would be alive today. They probably also wouldn't be such a scary problem."

Maia let out a heavy sigh, "Well, maybe they're all just lost souls who never found their way back. Maybe we just found the cure."

"Oh my God, alert the media!"

She actually crossed her arms and pouted. "I want to help her, but it is true that we can't just stay here forever. We can't wait that much longer."

I hated to admit it, but she was right. Bridget was staying quiet, keeping an eye from down the bond, but I knew it was weighing on her patience. If we were going to get a chance to talk to Maddie, it needed to happen now.

"Just give me a minute to think." My eyes were darting around the room. There had to be a way to help speed this up... Maybe we were just delusional and too hopeful...

"Bridget?"

"Hmm?" Bridget's response was like she'd just been waiting for me to cave. "Are you ready to come back now?"

"We just need a little more time. There has to be a way to help her wake up..." I bit my lip, looking up at Maddie. I wasn't quite sure I was ready for what I was about to ask. "Can I go into her mind and try to coax her back?"

Maia—who was listening into this conversation—whipped her head back at me, eyes wide. "Aly, you can't be serious!"

"I can go into Maia's head and she's not dead. I know we have the bond but is it possible?"

"Oh, umm... I hadn't thought about that." Bridget was thinking. This was good.

I put a hand up to silence Maia in her concern.

I understood where she was coming from, but now was not the time. If it was possible, this was our only chance.

"I'm not sure it'll work but if you really want to try, just don't spend too long in there."

"What happens if she spends too long?" Maia and her damned clarifying questions.

"Well, I'm not sure. This is a situation I haven't had before." Bridget admitted. "But if your stubborn sister can get herself out within, I'd say, no longer than ten minutes,

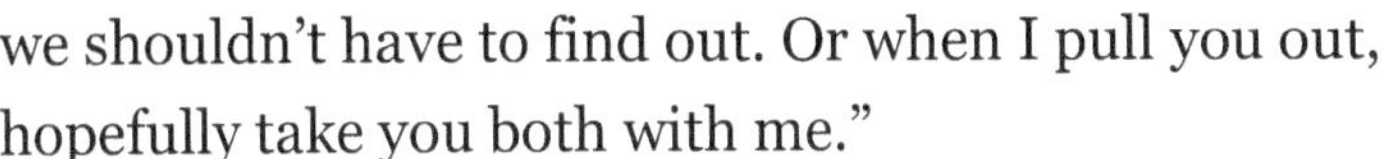

we shouldn't have to find out. Or when I pull you out, hopefully take you both with me."

"Hopefully?" Maia raised her brows. "That's comforting."

"Yea, well, hopefully it stays hypothetical."

I rolled my eyes, ignoring Maia, and stepped towards the bed. "No longer than ten minutes, that's fine. I only want a couple."

"Just get in and get out. Get it over with and don't ever roll your eyes at me again."

I already felt a nervous rush through my body. The adrenaline. I could do this. I could bring her back. Bridget kept telling me I was a bridge—what good was that if I couldn't do that now.

Maia was watching my every step as I neared the bed. When I had gone into Maia's mind I was holding her hand, pushing my energy towards her senses, her mind. I needed to feel Maddie. Sense her, not just see her. I needed to be one with her. Mesh my mind to hers. But she wasn't just an object I could move with my hands, so I got closer. Not to stand over her at the end of the bed, but join her at her side.

I also realized how creepy that would probably be to wake up to. You just talked to me and now I'm standing over you in a hospital room? That wouldn't go over well for me, I wouldn't do it to someone else.

Instead I took a seat with her. Slowly, as not to jolt her or shake the bed. She looked so peaceful laying there. All her time here had at least healed any remaining wounds, you'd never have guessed she'd fallen from a cliff, nearly to her death.

"Alright, Maddie. Here goes nothing, let's bring you home."

Focusing all my energy on Maddie, I slipped my fingers into her grip. I wasn't a detached soul, but somehow, something inside me knew who she was instantly. As soon as our skin met a chill ran up my spine, I felt my blood pulsing, and my mind began racing for the connection. My body knew who this was and what I was trying to do.

This was some crazy witch intuition I was gaining. Honestly—I could get high on this feeling.

My head was spinning, my mind searching for a way into hers—a door, a window, anything. Nothing was coming front and center. But I could feel a connection forming.

I pushed my hand further into her grip, trying to tighten the connection. Maybe she just didn't know it was me. Maybe when her mind was molding into this one it messed with the previous memories. That would make

sense when we weren't sure if she would remember The Crypt. But I had to find out.

I called out, "Maddie? Can you hear me? Can you see me?" And waited.

Please, she needed to let me in. I was so sure she was trying to wake up. Fighting for it. I could feel it. She just couldn't get through!

"Maddie!" Finally my mind rushed forward just as a door opened. Apparently my mind had a mind of its own. It saw the opportunity and dashed.

And there she was. Just like when I'm with Bridget and Maia, inside our bond. Maddie had let me in. Well into the dark gated area outside of her mind. But I was in.

"Maddie! It worked!" I wanted to rush to hug her I was so excited but her expression froze me, my arms dropping back to my side. "Wait, Maddie, why do you look so frightened?"

"I thought this was saving me..." Her lips were trembling, "But I got stuck... I don't know what happened. I can't wake up now."

"Maddie, that's why I'm here." I reached for her elbows —just a light touch of comfort, "I'm going to help you. You just have to trust me, ok?"

Finally, her head lifted and her eyes brightened, "How?"

"We don't have much time, but I have an idea—and it should keep your soul connected."

Her eyes instantly dulled again, "Aly, you need to know... I think there's something wrong... With my human self... She's not who I thought she was."

"Maddie, it's ok. We'll figure that out later. Right now, we just need to get you out."

"I saw memories..."

"Maddie. Look!" I was already focusing on my new portal. Just like the one I'd formed to bring her from The Crypt. "We need to wake you up. We need to make sure to get your human self safe and we don't have a lot of time."

Maddie had panic all over her face but I grabbed her hand. "Hold on tight and trust me. We're going through that portal."

She swallowed but nodded and gripped tighter.

"Now!"

"Aly?" I could hear Maia's voice calling to me. Was I back? I couldn't see her but I could hear her.

"Aly!" This time her voice came with a physical shake. "Aly!" Again, but this time was enough to pull me all the way back. The darkness around me finally cleared and I could feel again.

Blinking my vision clear, Maia was standing over me, next to the bed, but leaning close enough that I could feel her breath. Apparently in the process of diving into Maddie's mind my body had slumped across the rest of hers.

"It worked?" I said, rubbing my eyes, trying to clear the blur and fully see Maddie.

"You scared the living hell out of me!" Maia pushed me back just as I was pulling myself up, off of Maddie's still limp body.

"I'm sorry. I didn't know that would happen. How was I supposed to know what it would look like? But did it work?" We had no time for Maia's tense emotions right now, I was looking frantically at Maddie, searching for any sign of life coming back. "When I was coming back I had her with me. She should be waking up, any minute now."

We both paused, staring, waiting.

Seconds felt like minutes. Come on Maddie. I knew she was coming back to us. I had literally just dragged her back with me.

Then, Maddie finally gasped. Loud enough to send Maia and I both into the air like the climax of a scary movie, clutching our chests. Like watching the toaster—you know it's going to happen, you're literally waiting for it, yet it still scares you when it pops up.

"My God. Well it really took you long enough didn't it?" Having finally caught her breath from the not so easy wakeup call, now slumped back on her elbows.

"What?" Maia and I shared a confused glance. Those were her first words? "Took us long enough? Maddie, you can see us still? You know who we are?"

Suddenly, something didn't feel quite right.

"You remember?" I couldn't help narrowing my eyes at this Maddie, my anxiety was rippling. Her tone, her attitude, she can see us? Maddie's words echoed in my mind then, *she's not who I thought she was...*

Maia had tracked Maddie down to this hospital, but we were both still within the bond. We didn't know what she'd remember, let alone if she'd be able to see us. I hadn't actually even thought about that part. It wouldn't make sense now that we hadn't needed to physically come here.

"Yes, yes. I know. There's much to explain. But yes, to answer your questions—I can see you both, I remember you both, and I remember The Crypt."

This was definitely not the shy, coy girl we met by the pond in The Crypt...

"Do you remember what happened to you?" Maia's tone was also cautious. Bridget hadn't spoken up yet but her grip had already tightened on our bond. Ready to yank at any given moment—any suspicious word even.

"Yes." Maddie sighed, "Alright, don't hate me. I'm not a bad guy here. But what happened to me was planned. That man is not a part of anything anymore. He was barely a part of this." She tossed a hand as if she wasn't sure how best to describe him, "Collateral damage if you will. Not for him, he's fine... Physically... Just maybe some mental-emotional damage."

"What do you mean it was planned?" Now standing with Maia at the end of the bed, my fists were tightening at my side. Did we waste precious time on the wrong soul? Was this a joke? A trick? A trap?... A test? "Did you know where you would end up? You knew about The Crypt? How is that possible?"

"Yeah, also, if you knew about The Crypt and that you'd end up there... Why would you want that?" An even better point. Madam Detective, coming in trying to get to the motive.

"If you'd let me explain this will probably go a lot faster."

The gall.

"Well, by all means, please proceed." Raising my brows, I waved my hand in a guiding gesture.

I was so worried something might go wrong. I had such an inkling that something was just looming over us before we reached Maddie in the hospital room. Everything had gone so well up to this point. But this? I wasn't expecting this turn of events...

"I know you're both descendants of the Salem witches coven. Named after Martha and Alice. I know this because I am also a descendant of the coven. My ancestor betrayed the first witch..." She was looking straight ahead, now fidgeting her hands, clearly uncomfortable with the new

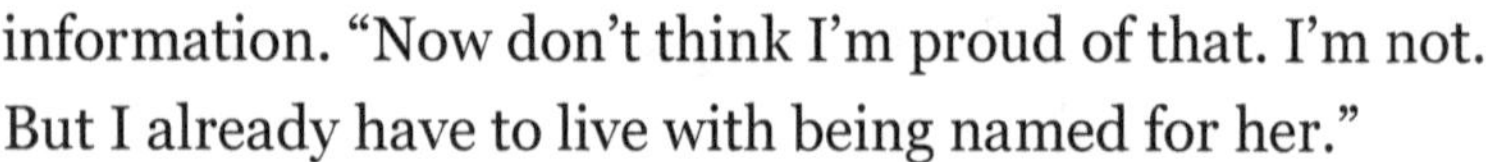

information. "Now don't think I'm proud of that. I'm not. But I already have to live with being named for her."

Her too. That's how it's known... What Bridget said from the beginning.

"I learned about this last year, when my 'accident' happened. Madam Selene came to me."

"Madam Selene is still here?" Bridget's shock finally came through the bond.

"She came to me, not because I was a chosen one but because of you two. She told me everything. Confirmed what I already suspected about myself and told me things I didn't. She said there were only two descendants and they needed to break the curse of The Crypt, but they were running out of time. You weren't figuring yourselves out quickly enough. She needed my help. I would also be your first test."

I couldn't even speak, gripping the end of the bedframe just to steady myself.

We had needed to make sure we could do more. We needed to know how far we could reach at once—see if we could open a door and save as many souls as possible rather than trying one at a time. This was our test... I knew this wasn't what Bridget had meant, but somehow Maddie had weaseled her way in? Had Madam Selene known we would do this? Or how did she figure it out?

"So what was in it for you?" Maia crossed her arms, her face looked like she was actually trying to understand this bullshit.

"As crazy as it may sound… She told me if I could help, she would help me with guidance on my new abilities and it would be redemption for my ancestor."

"Redemption?" Bridget's laugh burst in shock. "She wants to give that wicked witch redemption? Please!"

"Ok. Wait. But how did you know we would need to test our ability like this?" I put my hand up to pause everyone. "Also, you didn't find us. Bridget came to me in a dream. That's not exactly speeding up the process. Do you still get your end of the deal just because we brought you back?"

"Well, no. First. I did actually find you. I saw your light when you were talking to The Reaper. When you were still referring to him as 'the dark energy.' Remember another spirit popping in but that energy kept shutting it down? That's what made you dive deeper, wanting to know more. That's what opened the door for Bridget."

I blinked hard. "That was you."

"I needed to get the door open for Bridget and make myself the easy first target. Though, myself in The Crypt was a little difficult—she really was a different version of me. But luckily, I could stay as a voice in her head. Nudging her in the right directions."

"And you knew about this test… How?"

Maddie uncomfortably smoothed out her hospital blanket, not meeting our eyes now. "Aly. There are things I am not proud of. I needed to watch, wait, and learn…

When you're in my position, you figure out ways to learn plans..."

"So you were your own spy is what you're saying." I scoffed at her response, I wasn't holding back. I was fuming. It was taking everything in me not to shatter everything in the room.

"So all of this—for what? What now?" We still had to destroy The Crypt and save everyone. "Is this just over for you?"

"Well, see, you haven't let me finish." She paused to take a good look at both Maia and I, like she was truly taking both of us in now. "I found you, got things started, but to gain my guidance and ancestors redemption, I need to help finish it."

My jaw clenched at her words. Us team up now? With her? Like hell.

I don't know how Maia was staying so calm through all of this. She was just standing there, arms crossed, and her eyes narrowed on Maddie. But her expression was unreadable. Like disappointment but also trying to understand this girl—understand why she'd done what she'd done, was doing what she was doing.

"My ancestor is locked away, deep in The Crypt. Even separated from the other witches there. But she needs to stay there. She needs to be in that cell when The Crypt is destroyed and I need to make sure that happens. You need my help."

"Why wouldn't that happen regardless?" Oof, Maia did not like to feel challenged. Maddie made a mistake there.

"The Reaper has been looking for her. He knows if she's out The Crypt can't be destroyed without also letting her free."

Shit.

"Because we'll open the portal and she'll take the chance and run." I swore and put my hand to my temple.

"Exactly. You won't be able to stop her."

"Again, how do *you* stop it from happening?"

"Manpower." She threw her hands up like it was some obvious answer. "You need strength and numbers. And we need to do this soon."

"Manpower? That's why we're supposed to trust you now? Aren't you still learning—just like we are? And you've been in a coma for a year and now you're back after *we* helped you, but somehow *you're* the one running this mission now?" Maia tossed an accusing hand straight towards her. "No. Not that easy."

She did have a point though.

"I may still be learning, yes, but if you have to call on any ancestors still out there, it's much easier with more people. Whether we're all learning or we're all wise old witches already."

"I don't trust her." Bridget suddenly piped in again. "Her bloody ancestor turned me in out of pure pettiness. Who's to say she hasn't already released her and now she's just hiding out in The Crypt? She could just be waiting for her moment."

With my fingers drumming my arm, I looked back at Maddie. I'd begun to pace the room while we were talking, trying to make sense of all of this. "How can you prove anything you're saying right now?"

"She can't. We can't trust her." Bridget was chomping at the bit.

"Ok, Bridget, simmer."

"Bridget can go to her holding cell. I know where it is. I found it when I first got there. I searched for days."

"We aren't agreeing to anything until I see that witch locked up." I just knew Bridget was pouting—angry pouting at that, crossing her arms. But I also knew, on this, she wasn't budging. I wasn't going to push her. I wouldn't want to be pushed either.

"Can you connect through the bond? So when we do confirm, we can reach out."

"Now I should definitely be able to."

"Alright, we need to confirm what you're saying—see that she is locked up before we agree to anything."

Maddie closed her eyes and nodded, "I understand."

"So, where do we find her?"

Chapter 17

"We don't actually believe we can trust her, do we?"

"Of course not, I haven't completely lost my mind."

We were back inside the bond now, just the three of us. Again, surrounded by darkness, the only light coming from the soft glow between us. It used to be jarring. The sudden change from the world around you to nothing but a still glow. Now it was calming—a safe space.

"So what's the plan then?" Maia had clearly hit her limit. Honestly, fair. We couldn't trust Maddie anymore, but we still needed to look into what she had said.

"I need to go. I need to see. I don't trust her..." In that moment, that beat of a moment, Bridget's eyes glazed over. She realized who she was talking about.

Maddie had been her friend—a longtime friend. A sweet coy girl who showed up one day and had granted Bridget kindness. Friendship. That was seemingly lost now, all in the blink of an eye.

"I can't trust her anymore. But she may have been right. At least about a couple of things, including us needing her help."

"So we have to give her a chance to help if that witch is actually locked up?..." God I was dreading this uncertainty. So many things could go wrong.

"You know, I'm still not fully understanding why we need her help, even if the witch is locked up."

For once, I actually liked one of Maia's clarifying questions.

"All she said was 'manpower'." Maia made the quotation marks with her fingers, topped with a sarcastic face to match. "Does one more of us really make that much of a difference? What is she even going to do? Guard the cell so the witch can't get out? Be a distraction for The Reaper so he can't find it or something? I mean she's no match on her own. I don't get it." Maia was clearly not a fan of this intrusion.

Bridget only sighed and said, "Obviously I wish it didn't make any sense and that we could simply ignore it, but... Her added power could help strengthen not just Aly's but both of yours. While I'm stuck I don't have my full strength."

"So if we have the help, we need to use it... Even if we can't trust it." I cut in. I knew that's where this was going.

"Fine. But we need a plan in case something goes wrong. If we have to work together so that she can start on her little 'journey' to self-discovery and witchery and earn her weird, crazy ancestor some redemption, we need to make sure we're protected and what we need to do still happens."

"Yes, Maia. I agree." Bridget's light attempt to calm her before continuing. "But before we worry about a plan for that, I need to look into that cell. Creating a plan won't even matter if there is no witch that could even be released." Maia nodded in agreement and Bridget gave her hand a light squeeze before continuing. "Now. I'm going to release you both. You'll be back to normal and just prep as if we'd be moving onto next steps like normal. I will follow the exact instructions Maddie gave us—find the farthest, darkest corner of The Crypt. I'll report back after. But either way, remember, we will be saving the rest of these souls and you two need to get ready." Bridget took a pause, she'd been waiting to tell us something. "I've actually been thinking a lot about this and I think we need to go to a very special place to complete this." Now she was smiling.

Somewhere special? Figuratively? Physically? Why was she smiling? Wait...

"That is if you both can, but for this to be the biggest and largest connection—I mean, you are becoming the bridge for so many spirits. We could do it through the bond, but in person—the power together is massive! It would be so much easier."

"Where?" Maia's voice shook but she still looked excited. I couldn't completely read how she felt.

"Girls, we need to bring you back—to the place that gave you your names. To the place where if you need it, help will find you. Back to where it all started."

Bridget didn't even have to say it. Maia and I beat her to it and at the same time.

"Salem."

Coming out of the bond trance continued to be a bit disorienting. My soul wasn't being shoved back into my body thankfully, like going into The Crypt, but it was like getting control of your mind again. Like you had just come out of an out of body experience, a hypnotic trance. My mind was mine again.

Feeling around with my hands, I felt the bed sheets, the pillow behind my head. Yep, it was over.

After everything I wanted to be sure I knew where I was before even attempting to open my eyes.

But alas, rubbing them clear, I pushed myself up and looked back towards the couch where Bridget had been laid out. Gone now. Already off on her mission to find—I guess her now foe? She'd taken to calling her the wicked witch.

I really did hope she was in that cell. What could the alternative be? We just have to take the chance of releasing her? That was the plan before wasn't it? We didn't know she was ever locked in a cell. If she was, that would make our job and lives a whole lot easier. And obviously, Bridget happier.

But what if this was a trap? A setup. We never discussed what to do in that case. I knew Bridget could, in many ways, handle herself, but she said it herself, she's not as strong as she once was.

God, we really needed to get better at discussing all the possibilities! Everything we do seems to come with at least one thing we simply forgot or didn't think to discuss.

The thought alone worried me enough, I needed to at least get a quick message to her. Not distract her or call an emergency meeting. Just a warning.

"Bridget!" Gentle but desperate, still a whisper down the bond, even if it was maybe a yelled whisper. "I don't want to distract you, but I'm only just thinking of this now... Just be extra careful. This could also be a trap. If that happens, if you even get the sense, call to us. Remember what Maddie said before we left, 'Somehow he's got eyes everywhere.' Just be careful."

This was the first time I didn't hear a response. She was staying quiet. Focusing on listening to my words but not on speaking. Instead, she sent me a visual, I could see her nod to me, I felt her touch like a graze down my back. She understood, acknowledged and was thanking me.

That was wild.

I didn't know the bond could do that! Was it just getting stronger?

Shaking myself back, it was time to leave. The hotel was exactly what I needed. But now Bambi needed me. I needed a break from all of this too, and now I had to figure out how the hell I was supposed to explain needing to go to Salem to Wes.

Like, really? I just spent the night in a hotel cause I just wanted to get away. Now I decided I needed a few more days to maybe a full week away across the country. But don't worry—I promise I'm not leaving you. God.

"What the hell am I supposed to say? How do I explain that?" I had just gotten home and fed Bambi. I had a good amount of time, hours even, before Wes would be home, to figure this out. So I called Maia.

"Tell him you need a girls trip!"

"To Salem?"

"Well when you say it like that it sounds weird!"

"Because it does sound weird for a girls trip!"

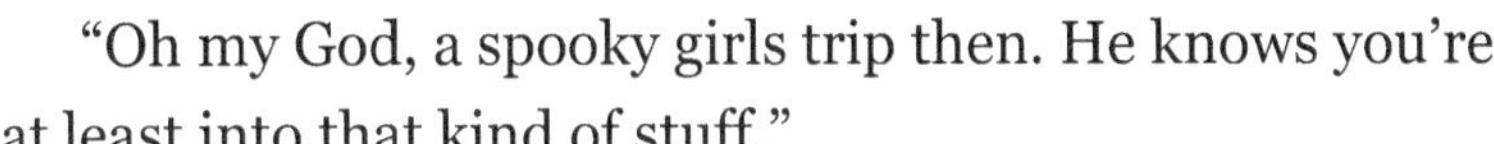

"Oh my God, a spooky girls trip then. He knows you're at least into that kind of stuff."

It's like she didn't even hear her own words sometimes. How random that sentence sounded out loud.

"Oh! I've got it!" I raised a brow, but was still listening.

"Tell him you want to come out for a visit and we're looking at making a trip out to Salem for inspiration or research for your book."

"Oh." That was a shift. "That actually might just work. That would make sense."

"Ha! See! Crazy enough that it just might work. I knew I'd think of something." Maia was delighted with herself.

Wes knew I had just started writing my first book. I had my business, but for months now I'd been working on a paranormal mystery. This trip would actually make sense. My book may not take place in Salem, but what better place for inspiration.

"I like it. However, he still might be thrown off by the quick notice."

"Eh, the night at the hotel was nice but made you realize you needed more. And you're missing family, what better mix!"

"You sound like you've really thought about this already..."

"I have. You can stay here obviously, and I've already looked at places in Salem."

Ok, now I was shaking my head, oh hell no. "Do you think we'll be there overnight?"

"I mean, we'll kind of have to be, it's too far from me—what were you thinking?"

"Uh..." She really had thought this out. I had barely walked through my front door when I called. "I mean, I definitely wasn't thinking I wanted to stay in the same town that we just released everyone in The Crypt, including our own coven. Even if some of those spirits are going to human bodies, um, our coven, and hopefully nothing evil."

"Eh, true—I guess I can look in the neighboring towns."

"That's probably better."

This girl was getting way too far ahead! I didn't even have a plane ticket yet.

"Do you think she's going to find her?"

"Huh? Who?"

"Bridget. Do you think she's going to find that cell? With the other witch."

"Oh." My stomach turned at the thought. At either result really. If she did find her, we had to work with Maddie. If she didn't... I didn't know what that would mean yet. "I don't know."

"I don't either—I'm just worried."

"Honestly, unfortunately, I think the only good option is for her to find her. So I hope she does. I just hate that we can't even trust Maddie anymore."

"I don't trust her, but what she said felt genuine. I like that even less."

"I feel the same way." I paused thinking about Salem again. "If she is telling the truth though, she can find her own way to Salem."

By the time Wes got home the day had passed and I had walked Bambi around the entire neighborhood trying to work out some anxiety.

I knew he wasn't going to have any sort of bad reaction, but how do you even bring something like this up and not expect questions? Questions were valid. Was it too hopeful to think he might just go with it and say to have a good time? If it was good for me and my writing, he was all for it?

Everything was a potential outcome and every one of them had me pacing the kitchen floor, biting my nails, when he walked through the front door.

Not exactly helping the 'act normal' look.

Putting my hand to my sides, smoothing out my already unwrinkled clothes, I came out of the kitchen.

"Hey!" I gave him a quick kiss hello as he was taking off his shoes. "How was your day?"

"Oh, nothing crazy, nothing new. Same people, same problems. How was yours?"

"It was good, actually. It was so nice out I decided to take Bambi all around the neighborhood. Discover some places we haven't been yet."

"Oh yea? You have a good day too buddy?" Wes leaned down to give Bambi a couple pats on the head. "I was also thinking, kind of feeling like ordering out tonight. Feeling like anything?"

"Sure, sounds good to me! Anything but burgers."

He just laughed and said, "Whatever sounds good, if you want to throw in an order. I'm going to change real quick and then you can fill me in on more of your night." Giving me another kiss he headed for the room.

Ok. I needed to remind myself to breathe. He just wanted to know that I got what I needed out of last night. It's the next topic. It's fine. Just breathe dammit.

"He's home. I'll let you know how it goes." I sent Maia the quick message.

"Already looking up flights."

Jesus. "Slow down lady! Calm down."

"I'm excited! You'll be fine."

"Soooo! How was it?" Wes was now rounding the corner to the kitchen. "Also, did you pick something to order yet?"

"Um... Not yet, uh, how about Chinese? We haven't had that in a while."

"Perfect. But the hotel, how was it? Where'd you go again?"

"Whispering Willow Lodge, it was actually really great." I turned to face him, leaning back against the counter. "It was definitely what I needed to get a little more creative and do some brainstorming. It was rustic but warm—it made you feel at home, not out in the wilderness. You could even say when it got a little later it had a bit of a spooky vibe."

"Well that's great babe." Wes was smiling at me now. He was always so supportive. One of the things I loved most about him.

"Yea, the brainstorming was actually something I wanted to talk to you about." I was going to put this as much onto Maia as possible. Her idea!

"Ok? What's up?" His brows were raised, but I had his attention.

"I called Maia while I was there, at the hotel. I was telling her that I was a bit stuck and could use some ideas. She came up with something and I thought it could actually help... She suggested I come out for a visit. She's so close to Salem—we thought we could do a maybe an overnight trip out there. We've both always wanted to go and now what better excuse than for some spooky fun, inspiration, and research for my book? I could go see family and get some work done. It's a win-win!"

"That's an interesting idea... And when did you want to go? Wait, does your book take place in Salem?"

"I know, it's spontaneous. But, if it's not crazy expensive, like next week? It doesn't take place there, but it would be for the research. I've been feeling so much more like a method writer lately. I need to go and see things, learn about them, understand them better to write about them." Dang, maybe this would help my writing. I was even convincing myself.

"I mean, if that's what you need, that's what you need babe."

"Really?"

"What? Am I really going to say no?"

"I was expecting you to say no while also expecting a yes, so yes."

That's when he finally came forward, arms outstretched towards me, putting his hands gently on my shoulders. When he realized that this was the only true way to convince me he was fine with something, I didn't know. But it worked every time.

"Go find a ticket, whenever you need to go, and have fun. I'll just be here. Just don't put any spells on me when you get back?"

I laughed but I could cry. He had a few questions, but ultimately my earlier wishful thinking wasn't so wishful after all. I was going to Salem. We were about to save a whole realm of spirits and our coven. Holy crap, we were going to meet our coven!

"No promises." I laughed about his spell comment. "Ok, let me order our dinner, go find something to watch."

"Just the usual?"

"Got it!"

Ah! I could hardly keep my feet from dancing. I was going to Salem!

Wait. Shit. Oh. My. God. I was going to Salem.

Once we were back I would tell him everything. I wasn't sure how he'd react but I'm sure he could handle it. But he just didn't need all of that right now. He'd just agreed for a whole different reason, why would I tell him now? No, when we got back. That was the right way to go. But of course, now I was curious and I couldn't help it.

"So, you said no spells on you when I get back. You didn't say in general." I raised a goofy eyebrow at him. "Really though, how would you react if I came home and had learned that I was a witch? I came home and can suddenly close doors and turn on the TV with my mind."

We'd finally gotten settled in for the night and our food had arrived. No burgers, no notes.

"Hey, if you're some kind of witch, that's fine. As long as anything you're doing is pointed at our enemies and not me, I'm good."

"You just assume I'm some sort of bad witch? What the hell?"

Well that was just offensive.

"No, no, I'm just saying." He made a sweeping motion with his hand. "Covering my bases."

"Uh, huh. Ok." But before I could say anymore, before Wes could respond, a loud smack crashed into the back window.

"The hell was that?"

The same I'd heard right before—another loud caw sounded, cutting off even my thought.

I was frozen.

The crash, the bird, last night at the hotel right after I'd gotten my food and that note... It couldn't be. This apartment was protected. But outside wasn't.

"Do you want me to go look?" Wes saw my concern.

"No, sorry, it's fine. It just sounded like something hit the patio maybe. I can peek." I couldn't risk him possibly finding some weird ass message—or worse... But now getting up I had to look normal. "Probably just a bird hitting the window." Totally normal. Why would I be expecting a demon carrier pigeon or basically a stalker outside our window?

Turning on the patio light, I peeked through the blinds first. No bird anymore, but a rock was left behind. Shit. A rock, with a string and a note? Another freaking note!

"What is it?"

"Uh..." Think! I couldn't just leave it, I had to grab it. "Uh, I'm not sure. Hold on." Sliding the door open slowly and taking a step out, I got closer. The bird had disappeared, back into the night. I took a couple steps closer to the edge, but I couldn't see anyone else anywhere.

No Reaper? Just a message? What did he want out of this? Bridget was still on her search and we hadn't heard from her yet, but he just shows up here?

I swore under my breath. I had to read that note... I at least had to grab it before Wes saw.

Doubling back from the patio's edge I snatched it from the ground. Whatever this was, I needed to talk to Maia and we needed to hear from Bridget.

"Hey babe, I just realized I haven't even told Maia that the plan is on yet. I really need to call her, do you mind?" I practically slammed the sliding door behind me, coming back in.

"Sure, what was the crash?"

"Oh, just a rock. I think a bird dropped it, but it didn't hit the window. All good."

"Huh, ok. Yea, I think I'm going to bed anyway. Have fun with Maia. Tell her I said hi."

"I will! Love you. Goodnight."

Hearing the door close behind him, I knew I was in the clear. I hadn't wanted to go back to my office, considering how I'd felt the last time in there, but I had no choice. If

Wes had gotten up for some water, I was screwed if I just hung out in the living room. It had to be the office.

I had the herbs, the sage, and one lavender candle I had left behind. That was all the protection I needed. I'd only taken it out to confine him to this space.

That was over now. There would be no place left for him. And only about ten minutes later, when I was done setting up, that was true. My mind was fully clear again. No irrational thoughts had come, no crazy wants, no feeling like I was going to vomit, no stiffness in the room, and no creeping chill like something was working its way into my mind. Nothing.

Finally... The note.

Maybe I should read it with Maia—call Maia first.

My hands were shaking, pulling at my phone.

"Soo? We're going right?"

"I can't be too loud, Wes just went to sleep."

"Ok, but we're going right?" I loved when Maia whispered over the phone like said person could hear her.

"Yes, we're going. As soon as possible. But I'm the only one who has to be quiet Maia, you're not on speaker." I quietly laughed.

"Oh duh, right. Ok, well great! I've already found some flights I'll send you! Also, have you heard from Bridget yet? I still haven't heard anything." She was talking a mile a minute.

"Maia, I love you, but you're going way too fast. I'm here. I haven't heard from Bridget yet, but someone else.

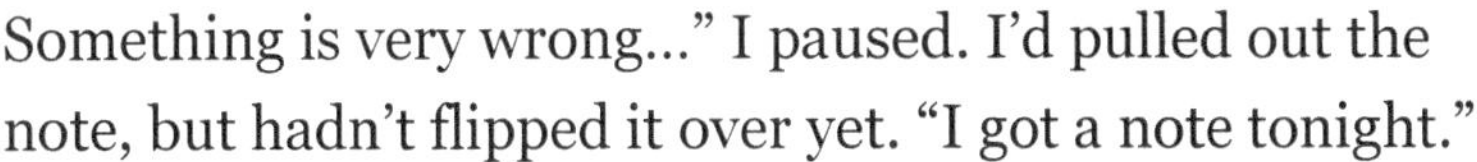

Something is very wrong…" I paused. I'd pulled out the note, but hadn't flipped it over yet. "I got a note tonight."

"A note?"

"I haven't read it yet—I think it's from him. I mean that's the only thing that makes sense. A crow dropped it on my balcony tonight."

"Umm… What?"

"It was tied to a rock."

"Well read it Aly. What are you waiting for?"

"I called you to tell you the plan was on and to finally read it! Ok. Something I'd prefer to not read by myself. Jeez." Slowly turning the note in my fingers, I just stared at the words.

"Aly?"

"Always watching — Signed The Reaper."

Maddie's message.

"Bridget…" We both just barely whispered.

Then something more strange started to happen. The words started disappearing.

"Wait—What the—?"

"Girls?" Bridget's voice. Finally she was coming through the bond. "Girls?"

"Yes! Yes, we're here!" Maia shouted.

"Oh goodness. Girls. It's true. I found her."

Chapter 18

"It was true?"

The note—the vanishing message—guess that would have to wait.

"Selene must have come through even more than I thought. That witch had already come for me once, I wouldn't have been surprised if she'd tried something in the afterlife too. I always thought she was just pouting somewhere pathetic."

"Where are you now?" I didn't want to put her on edge, but after that note, I needed her paying attention.

"Um, I think I'm finally close to the clearing now. I'm going to my shack to prepare. I've been trying to reach you both, but that part of The Crypt is cut off from the bond. That witch has been living in complete isolation."

Damn. Madam Selene was not messing around. She really did a number on that one. Not just The Crypt, not even just locked in a cell, complete cut-off.

"Aly's coming to stay with me! While you were on your mission we nearly completed ours. We just need to get her flight worked out."

"For Salem?"

"I guess we're helping Maddie after all."

"Oh, I wasn't expecting even more good news!" I'd never heard Bridget so giddy. "Well, not the Maddie part. But Salem! You'll both get to see your true roots. I wonder how much it's changed." It was in her voice, her mind was starting to wander off.

"We'll let Maddie know about the plan but I already told Maia, she can find her own way there."

At this point, I didn't care who she was or what she was doing for us, I wouldn't spend a second longer than absolutely necessary. Who knew what genes her ancestor had passed down.

"Play nice girls, we can use her now. I have to too."

"Your betrayal is locked in a cell. You don't even have to talk to it!"

"I meant with Maddie."

"Oh."

"So just play nice. This will all be over soon." There was finally relief in Bridget's voice—not just in the plan

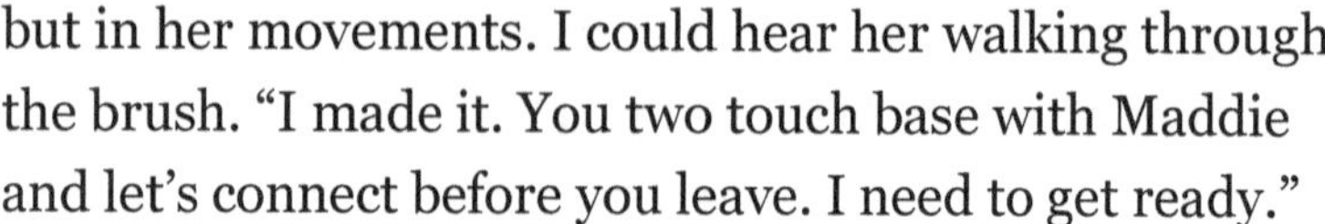

but in her movements. I could hear her walking through the brush. "I made it. You two touch base with Maddie and let's connect before you leave. I need to get ready."

Then she was silent.

Everything was happening so fast. It was only this morning that I got home from the hotel... How did Bridget find the cell so fast? I guess Maddie was the one who did all the searching—she told Bridget exactly where to go. How was it that good of a hiding spot?

Still, so fast. Now we were uprooting to Salem...

"Aly?" Huh? Was Maia saying something? "Aly!"

I snapped back, we were still on the phone, "Huh? Sorry."

"Earth to Aly!" Snapping her fingers in the background.

"Sorry! A lot's going on. I spaced out a second, sue me."

"It is a lot. I get it. Sorry, wasn't trying to be snappy, you just like... Really zoned out there. I think we both need to get some sleep."

"Alright. Elephant in the room. How do you want to do this?"

Maia went silent. She clearly was not ready to speak another word to that girl yet—but why me?? I really didn't want to say what I knew I'd probably have to.

The silence hung between us another minute. I wanted her to break so bad. Just this once, Maia! Break!

Ugh, I couldn't take it. I wasn't going to be happy about it, but I knew she wouldn't do it. "Fine. You owe me, Maia."

"I'll work on the Salem plans!"

"Remember, I still need to work out plans for Bambi too. This isn't just overnight, it's days. I can't be on a plane first thing tomorrow morning."

"Yes, of course. You just worry about... That." By her tone I just knew she was waving her hand as if shooing a fly away. "I'll send the other details—obviously for you to confirm."

I begrudgingly agreed and hung up.

It's funny, Wes thought I was using the hotel for a night away for stress relief—and in one sense I was, I could not have handled staying home last night. But stress relieved? I felt more exhausted from the stress than ever. Like a bus had just plowed into me.

Slumping back into my chair, I couldn't just fall asleep yet. Not without dreaming...

A drink. That's what I needed right now. The only good bottle we kept in the apartment—that I never drank, and some time to just think.

I knew things needed to move quickly. We had literal souls relying on us, whether they knew it or not. Without us they became more victims of The Reaper and whatever evil was out there that he answered to. But this plan... This need... Everything had turned into so much more. Only a few weeks ago Maia and I were squealing over a flashlight, now we were keeping souls from being eaten by some dark entity?

I took the shot I'd poured myself. Wes' Mezcal—he wouldn't notice a shot or two gone. It was the good stuff too. The one I could actually stomach.

I knew I had to face the fact that our lives were already changed forever, but this was even more. Now we might also have to deal with how Maddie fits into all that. God! Why'd we have to catch a stray in all this shit too!

What the hell did Madam Selene even mean by promising her guidance? She was permanently deleting her ancestor. Did she assume Bridget would step in to teach her? That couldn't be it... In reality, Maddie probably didn't even know the answer yet. Selene promised guidance and her word was all she needed.

Now my only decision was to keep spiraling and try to sleep or take one more shot, pull the trigger, and just deal with it.

"Screw it. Might as well." I downed one more shot. "Here goes nothing."

I didn't have to project my mind to the hospital or track her back down. I just needed to call her through the bond. I could do that. I'd done it with Bridget plenty of times—never with someone living—but how different could it be?

Leaning back in my chair I tried to get in a calm meditative mood. Focus on the warmth from the drink, the quiet and stillness of the apartment. Wes was asleep but nothing needed to be spoken aloud. This time of night you'd normally hear the smaller critters and birds scurrying across the roof. Tonight, it was like even they knew something was happening.

My mind was just about clear when a creeping thought of that note poked back in. That damned note! Not just what it said, but the letters, the words, why did they disappear? It had the same message Maddie had said to us... Could she know anything about that?

I knew we couldn't trust her, but she did tell us about the cell. Could she really be partnered up with The Reaper? It couldn't be that bad... That conniving... That planned. That would be such a long game. Then again, she had been in a coma for a year.

No. No. She might understand but that was too much. I was getting ahead of myself.

She'd be there if we needed the help.

I let my eyes close, "Maddie?"

"You made it! Does that mean you found her?"

My eyes rolled even while closed. It was that subtle, *I told you so,* in her tone—really pissed me off.

"We found her."

"So what's next? We can't let her out, but I have to help you. Please." She took a strange pause. "I really do want to help. Not just for myself. That miserable place *needs* to be destroyed and I truly do want to learn."

I hated that she sounded genuine.

Bridget said to play nice. I could do that. But now it was just the two of us. I could either fully play into the idea of believing her and that everything was fine. The less believable option. Or help her understand where she truly stood.

I didn't like games and I really was not down to play right now.

"Maddie. You were a completely different person inside that world. I don't know if it was all just a facade..."

"It wasn't..."

"Or..." Ignoring her cut-off, "If that person we knew really is somewhere in there. Buried as deep as she may be. That was our friend, especially Bridget's, and we want

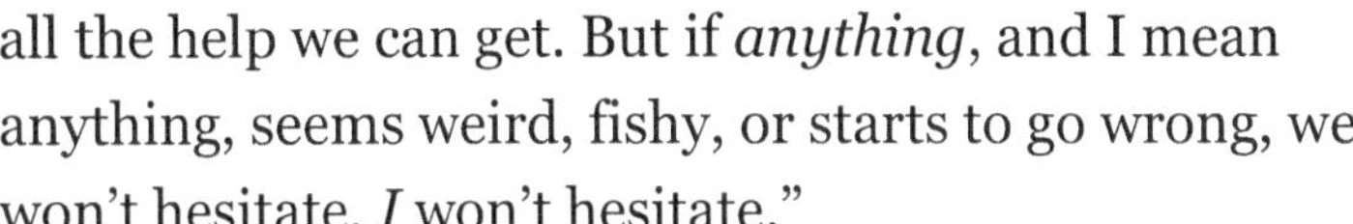

all the help we can get. But if *anything*, and I mean anything, seems weird, fishy, or starts to go wrong, we won't hesitate. *I* won't hesitate."

"I understand."

"I'll throw you back into The Crypt myself if I have to." She didn't laugh, good decision on her part. She knew I was serious. "So two things are next. To perform the connection to free all the souls, we need to go to Salem. We're figuring out when. We'll let you know. But if you want to help, be there."

"Salem, ok great."

"Number two. I got a note tonight. From him. It was the same message you warned us with before Bridget went looking for the cell. But the message disappeared right after I read it. Would you know anything about that?"

"Is this the first one you've gotten?"

"No. There was one other last night."

I couldn't see any of her expressions, but she paused briefly, "Did a crow bring it?"

"Well the first time a crow flew into the window after I got it with room service. But this time... Yea..."

"You said it was the same message as I'd given you?"

"Yes."

"Mmm. That crow, Aly. That's how he does it, how he knows everything... I don't really know if he has more than one, I've only seen one. It flies around The Crypt keeping watch."

Keeping watch?? How did I never see a single crow? Wait...

"The crow lives in The Crypt, but it can get out? Like some delivery pigeon?"

"That I didn't know. But if it can leave and brought you notes, it can probably bring anything."

Was that message because he knew what we did with Maddie? Or... Bridget. Bridget was in there when we got it and he didn't show up with this one. I thought it was a taunt—something to scare us. Was it a warning?

"I got this last message while Bridget was still in The Crypt. I'm not sure how long after it was, but I got it after she'd found the cell. She'd already made it back, close to the clearing."

Maddie sighed. "Well that's not great, but you definitely need my help for this one."

"You know, you keep saying manpower is what we need. We were going to do this without you from the start so please explain what you really mean."

"I get it. I do. You all pretty much hate me at this point and I don't blame you."

I rolled my eyes again. She's seriously trying to get empathy from me? Just explain yourself for crying out loud!

"On with it, Maddie."

"When I say that, I mean your ability to create that bridge is already strong. I know it is. I've already gotten to feel it. Maia the tracker, you're the bridge, and you can think of me for now as—the boost."

My brow furrowed, "The boost? Again. Explain."

"Using me will make you both stronger. Your bridge will be larger and Maia's tracking will be faster. She will be the guide for the souls you're connecting. Plus, if I'm still not enough, we can call on the coven together, they can still help. Don't you understand Aly? You'll be drawing strength from me! From my energy because we're from the same coven."

"We can call on them? Through the bond?"

"Obviously, how else would we?"

Didn't need the snark, jeez.

"We're freeing them from that hellhole too, but I'm not completely sure what their strength is at now. Just like Bridget said, her strength isn't what it used to be."

"Alright." I knew this was for a greater purpose but God did it pain me to agree to anything with her now. "Well I guess it's settled. You need us and we need you. Do you have any protections?"

"Protections?"

"You started practicing before your 'accident' and you don't have any herbs or crystals? Anything?"

"Oh…"

I put my head in my hands, "Get some. You'll need those, especially for traveling. It should keep The Reaper off your trail. The last thing we need is him tracking you directly to us before this all goes down."

"Say no more. Hey we both learned something new."

"Mm." I grimaced at even having that in common. "And I'll reiterate this once more—I sense something even slightly weird is up, it's done."

"You have my word."

I wish that meant more.

"Figure out your own travel. We'll see you in Salem in a few days."

"Aly. Hold on."

"There's nothing else Maddie." But I did still wait.

"You don't have to trust me yet, but just know. Selene doesn't step in for no reason. She showed me what could be and what needed to be stopped. This may not have been the best way, but at the time, it felt like the only way."

"I'll see you in Salem, Maddie."

I opened my eyes before she could say another word. Looking down, I hadn't even realized I was gripping the chair armrests.

Showed her what could be and it needed to be stopped. She had to be talking about The Crypt, The Reaper, what was happening—but why would she mention that? What else could it be? What did we not know? She was acting like some grand magic puzzle piece we needed to save the day and we just didn't know it yet.

Showed me what it could be. Over and over, now the phrase wouldn't stop. It was like a broken record in my head... Why were there so many damn secrets?!

Then I stopped. She was already getting in my head.

I didn't care what she meant. We'd figure it out sooner or later anyway. Shit, I needed sleep.

"It's done. She'll be in Salem." I texted Maia, finally climbing into my own bed. It was done and I couldn't even feel happy, sad, or angry about it. I was just over it.

"Yay." So was Maia.

Chapter 19

Ping! Ping! Ping!

"Oh God, five more minutes!" I slammed my hand on the bed before rolling towards my nightstand. "Who could possibly need something this early?"

I snatched my phone to look at the blindingly bright screen.

Oh. Maia. Then I saw the time. Shit! It was already 8 AM? God, my head hurt. Thanks to that Mezcal I'd woken up to a raging headache that pounded with every ping.

Ping!

"Ughhh... I should not have had that extra shot..."

At least twenty unread messages from Maia. One from Wes. At least he was saying good morning.

I'd apparently slept through every set alarm and him leaving for work. I felt bad but at least his message made me smile.

"Alright, Maia, I get it." I put my phone down. I just needed a minute of peace—or at least some semblance of it. I couldn't even be in my own home until last night. If it weren't for this headache I would've been grabbing a pillow and screaming into it. Coffee and a good scream. That's what I needed.

"It's fine. Just a little longer." I just stayed laying there, staring at the ceiling. "Just a little longer and this will all be over. The souls and coven will be freed, The Reaper will be gone, and then we can move on with our new life. Breathe." Sensing the stress and me finally waking up, Bambi came in a rush from under the covers. Poking her head out, her eyes wide, looking right at me to see if she was right. I couldn't help but laugh.

I'm pretty sure she's the only dog I've ever seen wake up with bed head thanks to those long floppy ears. Her ears were the only thing that were already so big when she was a puppy that they never got any bigger. She had to grow into them. Adorable honestly. I fell in love with her as soon as I saw them.

"Well good morning, are you ready for a late breakfast?"

That was all she needed to hear. Using me as a springboard, she launched herself towards the end of the bed and trotted down her stairs.

"Ok, well geez. Give me a second, you didn't have to gut punch me." Man, everyone's rushing me now.

But Bambi had no patience for me or my headache. Payback for leaving her for even just one night. I wasn't allowed to do that. I was really going to have to make up for Salem. Maybe I could find her a cute little witchy dog toy to bring back.

"Bambi, I guess you might be my familiar now." I told her while pulling on some normal clothes. Jeans and a T-shirt today would suffice. Bambi just tilted her head at me, waiting for a word she knew.

"Do you want to be my familiar?" I smiled at her. "You really don't care as long as you get breakfast huh?" Yea, that's when she started hopping.

"Yea, yea, I know. Ok, let's go."

Normally when I wake up it's still crisp outside. Too chilly to have my coffee on the deck in the shade. Too dark for Bambi's morning walk. Now? Perfect timing.

"Sorry I missed you." I sent Wes a quick text while serving Bambi her food. Maia could wait a little longer, she'd live.

"Umm, hello?" Or not. I almost didn't respond.

"Give me a minute. I have a headache and it's really nice out. Just let the Tylenol kick in first. Please?"

"You're lucky. I was about to come through the bond."

Geez, I knew we were booking tickets and making plans, but can't a girl sleep in a little bit?

She sent one more message, "You have one hour." Whatever, I'd take it.

"Finally! Alright, are you ready?" Maia was way too cheerful for this head to handle.

I'd settled myself on the couch with Bambi now. She was fully fed and ready to cuddle. I was laid back with an ice pack on my head, still waiting on the Tylenol's full effect.

"Two things. I know you're excited, but please, my head, can we bring it down a couple of notches please? And two, you sent way too many messages this morning— I read none of them."

"Wowwww... What happened to 'Thank you Maia, for putting in all that time and energy to plan and figure out our trip!' Where'd that go?"

"I talked to Maddie last night."

Maia gave a short pause. "Touché."

"Also, have you heard from Bridget?"

"No, but she said to reach out before we left. I figured she's waiting on us."

"Yea, I guess that's true. I don't know, just not very like her not to check-in if we're not moving fast enough. She's in a hurry." I also couldn't stop thinking about that crow. I hadn't mentioned it to Maia yet, but I needed to know Bridget was still ok.

"She's getting prepared, same as us. I'm sure she's fine, now pay attention." She snapped her fingers at me over the phone. Always making noises like I could see her...

But my mind was still elsewhere—the headache was finally starting to fade and Maddie's words began creeping back in, so I just let her proceed while my mind wandered.

He used that crow to keep watch. Used it to deliver messages for him. It wasn't very smart though. I mean, it flew into the damn window once and just tossed a rock another time. But still, there were no other animals in The Crypt. I had to be missing something.

Then, the realization jerked me upright, gasping...

"Is it him?! Or an extension of him?"

"Huh?" I'd cut Maia off mid-sentence. "Aly, are you even listening?"

"Maia! It's him! Sorry, the plan sounds great. But we need to talk to Bridget."

"What's him? The note? We already knew that. What are you talking about?"

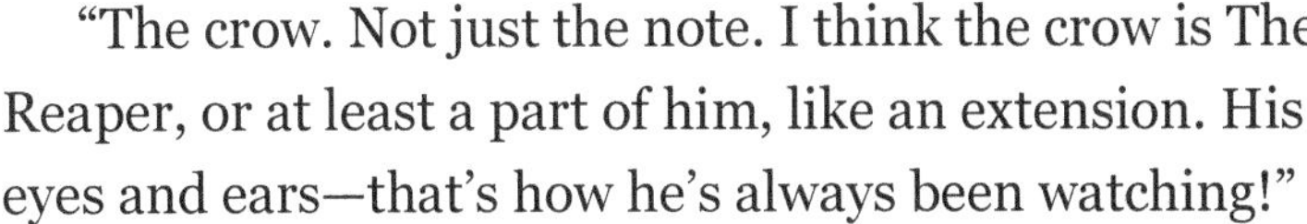

"The crow. Not just the note. I think the crow is The Reaper, or at least a part of him, like an extension. His eyes and ears—that's how he's always been watching!"

"Did you see it again?"

"No, but we also haven't heard from Bridget."

I didn't wait for another word, I was already sending a silent signal down the bond. I needed her attention. But nothing came back.

"Bridget?" I whispered this time. "Are you there?"

My chest was tightening, my heart racing the longer that pause lasted. Maybe she didn't hear me.

"Bridget!" I tried to whisper scream it.

Still nothing. Then finally, Bridget's voice broke through the tense silence. "Girls?"

"Bridget! You're ok! Oh, thank God."

"Girls, I'm ok, but did you talk to Maddie?"

"I did, she's meeting us in Salem. Maia and I were just discussing plans and were going to reach out."

"We're leaving in the morning." Maia piped through.

Oh shit, I guess I should've been paying closer attention.

"Uhm, I don't think Maddie's meeting us in Salem anymore."

"Why?" That shifted my tone. Had she already proved to stab us in the back? That quickly?

"She's here. In The Crypt. She's back."

"She's what?"

"You know I can feel when someone is entering and leaving this place. My senses were practically burning this time. I knew it wasn't one of you two and it wasn't him. It was someone new. I went to the clearing and there she was."

"Did you talk to her?"

"Not yet. I didn't know if you'd been able to see her yet about the plans. I still don't understand why it felt so different. It was her, but also someone else entirely. Almost as if the Maddie we knew before and this new Maddie are two completely different people."

Suddenly the pieces were coming together. But I had to think quickly.

"I did talk to her…I have an idea, but can you stay hidden until we're in Salem?"

"I think so, yes."

"Just stay away from that clearing and away from Maddie. I'll explain later."

What was going on?! How was Maddie back in The Crypt?... This didn't feel right. I didn't think Bridget was lying, but how was that possible? And she wasn't the old Maddie—the one we all, not just knew, but came to love in The Crypt. She was *this* Maddie? The one we brought back?

Part of me wanted to jump back to that hospital room to see for myself, but my gut was telling me no. I had an idea, I just had to be patient. Not my strongest suit, but fine.

Either way, Maia and I knew we had to move fast. She trusted me to take care of our plan for Maddie and she got everything booked. Connecting with Bridget only changed one tiny detail last minute. Instead of leaving in the morning, I'd be on a red-eye that night.

Wes was a little surprised by the urgency but once I explained, "We found a better deal. Plus this works out better because Maia's work friend will be in town tonight so she'll be able to get right over to Bambi." He was pretty easily on board.

"Ok, whatever you want to do babe. I'm on board."

It was also already booked and he was still confused— but I'd worked it out and I was excited so he let it go.

This did work out better though. Maia's friend already knew Bambi and she was coming to town for work. She'd be coming by to help and it ended up lining up perfectly with the trip. So with that settled, I was off—crystals, herbs, and literally anything else I could think of, on hand.

The trip to see my family was always long and exhausting—red-eye or not. There were no direct flights. But what that did mean was that I had the next nine hours to plan.

Freeing the spirits and destroying The Crypt—that was on Bridget... But this? Questioning Maddie even more—her loyalty, her intentions, her life even. Most importantly, was she now or has she always been working with The Reaper?... There were so many questions, all of them on me to find an answer.

If we were wrong... If she wasn't working with him and he had in fact killed her, did we unknowingly lead him directly to her?

There was no way...was there?

If he had learned of our plans... were we really able to draw so much energy from her? Is that why it mattered so much? That would be enough to kill her and send her back to The Crypt?

Bridget said it felt like a new person when she first felt Maddie coming into The Crypt. Sitting on that plane, I was really questioning my decision not mentally jumping back to the hospital to check on her. But how would I have explained myself? If she could somehow come and go from The Crypt, and then woke up to me. I couldn't exactly explain myself without letting anything be obvious that we knew.

No, now I knew I made the right decision. No option was truly good enough. All I knew now—if Maddie wanted to be back in The Crypt so bad, I'd put her back myself.

As the second plane was finally landing, I was finishing my plan to do just that.

"Just getting out! Are you here yet?" I texted Maia as soon as I was walking out of the airport. I was so ready to be on the road and at the hotel. I hadn't even had a chance to really see where she'd chosen to stay, I was just ready for a comfy chair and bed after that plane ride.

"Ahhhhh! I'm coming around the corner now!" The excitement of coming together again—like we weren't on our way to destroy some soul sucking, evil, crypt keeper.

But seeing Maia in person never felt like any time had passed. To think, I almost convinced Bridget to not include her in this final plan... Now, I didn't know if I'd have survived the trip without her.

Just as I was reading her text, I looked up to see her Jeep Renegade, in fact rounding the corner—Maia waving and doing a little dance from the driver's seat.

"Get in, get in! Throw the bag in the back." She called out the window as she pulled up directly in front of me.

"I'm going, I'm going." Quickly tossing in my carry on and climbing in.

"Did you get the plans ready?"

"Oh, jumping right in then huh?" I'd barely had time to settle in and even get my seatbelt on. "No, 'Hey, how was your flight? Was the food good?'" I had to chuckle at myself as she pulled through the airport traffic.

"Oh we both know the flight sucked, it's too long and exhausting, and the food is like crackers, chips, or a cookie." She wasn't wrong.

"Well I can't share the plans yet. Not without Bridget and we need to set up the room first." I wasn't taking any risks. "You brought protections, right?"

"Uhm, duh? We're going up against some dark lord demon. You really think I'd forget those?" She said it sarcastically but still looked slightly offended at the suggestion.

"My bad, just double checking." I held my hands up in defense. "How long till we're there?"

"Not long, only about 2 hours."

Luckily, it was early enough that by the time we were on the road there was no traffic and the drive was beautiful. Washington is pretty, where I had come from, but this is something different. There's more than ugly freeways everywhere and you still get freeway speeds in most places. So the whole way we got to enjoy long stretches of fields, gorgeous forests filled with trees changing colors with the season, and cute historical homes. No home looked brand new—maybe a few updates here and there, but you could tell they were all at least a hundred years old.

"So, I'm sorry, I still haven't had a chance to see where we're staying."

Maia gave me a sideways disappointed glance. "Give me your phone."

"You're driving." I narrowed my brows at her.

"Just gimme. I don't even have to look and we're coming up to a light." I slowly handed her my phone.

When she came to a stop she quickly went to my messages, swiped specifically on her name and hit delete.

"What was that for?"

"I sent you hotels to look at. I sent you what I chose, and you had the whole plane ride and a layover to look. You had your chance. Now it's a surprise."

The hell?

"I'm sorry, I've been a little busy. You know, I had to figure out a plan to deal with someone who's apparently potentially already stabbing us in the back and trying to ruin this whole thing."

"And you're making me wait to hear that too."

I hated when she had a point.

"Fine. Fine. We're getting close anyway. How far outside of Salem are we staying anyway?"

"Umm... Not far." I noticed a bit of hesitation and her pitch went slightly higher. "Speaking of Maddie, have you heard anything? Nothing's come through for me. I figured if she said anything it would come through for both of us but I'm still trying to figure out how our bond works outside you and Bridget."

"Nope. Not a word. But if she shows up, I don't think we'll hear until tomorrow. I told her a couple days. Which turned out better than I thought. We need the time today."

And we'd need the time. I needed the rest and we needed time to connect with Bridget. Poor Bridget was still hiding, waiting for our word.

"Wait, are we already here?" That drive felt a lot shorter than I expected.

"Almost!"

"No no, I mean in Salem. Are we in Salem?"

"Mmhmm." Maia was smiling. I was a little confused but maybe we had to drive through Salem to get to the hotel.

"I don't know what I was expecting. It all looks like it's changed but tried not to change at the same time."

I couldn't help but look around in awe. Such sadness, deception, and betrayal had taken place in what had turned into such a beautiful, historical little town. Passing a sign directing you where to go for the Witch Dungeon Museum had made me realize where we were.

"Wait, what are you doing?" I'd been too distracted by the town I hadn't noticed Maia turning to park.

"Parking." She said, leaned back and waited. This was my surprise.

"Maia… The Hawthorne??" I stared in shock. We were parked in front of the famous Salem hotel. "You chose, of all places, The Hawthorne, *in* Salem? What happened to outside of Salem?"

"Changed my mind." She shrugged and couldn't keep the giddy grin off her face. "Oh, it'll be fine. I was thinking —if we're freeing the witches who are supposed to be from our coven, it's not very welcoming to just run away after. Who knows, it could be a nice new home for their spirits."

"It's already haunted, Maia."

"So they can make new friends. Come on, grab your stuff. We don't want to keep Bridget waiting."

Chapter 20

"See, I knew you couldn't be mad once you were inside." Maia had caught me staring in awe at quite literally everything. I couldn't help it. I'd been thinking about this hotel since the first time we'd talked about making a trip to Salem years ago. Then, of course, it felt like fate when a couple of our favorite online ghost hunters also stayed at this hotel.

"No, I'm not mad... I just—with what we're about to do, and now with Maddie especially, having the escape route farther than just down the street was comforting."

"Aly. I'm still here and we have Bridget. Everything is going to be fine. We're about to destroy a whole— dimension? And take down The Reaper? I think we can

handle a few extra ghosties, a wicked witch, and another little stupid wench if we have to.”

Fine, that got a laugh. “Wench?”

“What else should I call her? We already have a wicked witch!”

“True, I guess that works. Alright, alright. We need to get set up so we can call in poor Bridget. She’s still hiding out in her shack.”

Our room was surprisingly simple compared to the rest of the hotel. When you think of a hotel that’s over a hundred years old, you might imagine creaking floors, old walls that would give you a splinter, and ceilings looking like they’re about to cave in. Not here. This hotel was grand.

Every inch had been refinished, retouched, and polished but not modernized in the slightest. I already knew we’d be back.

Our room luckily had a wonderful view overlooking the town. It may not have been quite as grand as the rest of the hotel but it was still cute and cozy.

Two updated queen beds and two thatcher-style armchairs directly across set with a nice glass table in-between. An additional small oak wood desk sat against the wall directly next to the bathroom door—an extra room mirror hanging on the wall next to it. Nothing more than we needed.

“Lavender, chamomile, crystals, salt...” Maia pointed at each item as she took note. We didn’t have our normal bowls for everything but we'd both had to pack for traveling, so easy pouches worked instead. "Are we forgetting anything? I feel like we're forgetting something." She said, drumming her fingers to her chin.

"I think that's it. I think this is as much as we can do. I also did bring some sage for after too. Once we leave we can cleanse."

"Oh good, ok." Maia stood there a moment, staring at our prepared table. "It's really happening. We're really trying to destroy some demon hell tonight..."

I only nodded, tightening my lips. Every step closer was growing more and more real. Neither one of us had still fully processed.

"We can't mess this up." Maia finally turned to me.

"I know. We won't. Breathe. Don't focus on that—just come here and let's call in Bridget."

"Well you two sure dress the part." Bridget observed from her now slumped position in one of the chairs across from us. She looked exhausted from hiding.

Maia and I were both currently in leggings and sneakers—Maia with her favorite purple oversized hoodie, and me in a gray half-zip pullover.

"We brought clothes for later… I was just on a plane for nine hours and then we were in the car for two more." I looked from Maia back to Bridget. "Should we have worn our best Victorian gowns for check-in?"

Maia clicked her tongue and swatted a hand, as if shooing away my comment like a fly. "We're saving our best clothes for when we meet our coven."

"Oh, I'm just joking, it really doesn't matter. I do hope you brought something black but it won't ruin anything."

"Black anything?" I raised a brow.

"A black dress is tradition for any sort of ritual, but that's all it is. Unfortunately, a lot of tradition doesn't really exist anymore."

I gave Maia a quick look—she nodded in return. We were wearing those black dresses we'd brought. Just in case.

"Bridget? Are you ok?" I dipped my head to look at her from the bed. She'd begun staring off. I knew she had to be thinking about Maddie… Two betrayals by two good friends. All while she gave so much. "Bridget?"

"Yes, yes. I'm good. We should begin, there is much to do." Snapping herself back, she reached for the bag she'd managed to bring with her. "First—speaking of traditions, I do have gifts for you both."

Reaching into her bag, I was expecting maybe some sort of memento from The Crypt—maybe something from Salem in the past. But no, I was not expecting the two beautiful wands she withdrew and now held on display.

"This is tradition for coming of age, your rite of passage. They were crafted for each witch in the coven." Gently, she handed the first to Maia. It was stunningly carved and smoothed out with gold wrapping the handle in a thin spiral around a clear quartz crystal. Absolutely perfect for Maia.

"Typically there is more of a ceremony, but we're obviously in a bit of a different situation."

Gazing at the wand, still laying flat in her hands, all Maia could get out was, "It's beautiful."

"That one has the clear quartz. It's meant to amplify your intentions. And Maia, we discovered that you're a tracker, but I sense more than that. I know this wand will help us truly determine your greatest strengths. Now, as for you Aly."

Maia still hadn't moved her hands or her gaze. Still fully taking in this new gift and what it meant.

"Aly, this one is for you." This one was not smooth, quite the opposite actually. It didn't have a crystal handle, but it was also absolutely perfect. She handed me what almost looked like a mini walking stick. It had a few rough edges and a handle that curved into what looked like a subtle claw—or at least how a claw would look at the end of a branch.

"The handle on this one is representing cradling the night. See how it looks like a full moon with the star?" I was nodding along. "It's harnessing the night. That dash of color coming down the side, that's melted amethyst. Meant for protection and powered by moonlight."

"Bridget, these are incredible." I needed to figure out where to keep this.

"Like I said, there is normally a ceremony but I wanted to make sure you both got them. When you grow up within the coven, they are crafted for you specifically. But when the trials were happening and I was already in The Crypt, Selene came to me. Your ancestors were going up to trial and Selene already knew then who you'd both be connected to. She came to me with their wands for safekeeping."

"You're saying these are basically heirlooms?" She simply smiled and nodded.

I was holding the wand that my ancestor used before being put on trial... Now that didn't feel real.

"Oh, and I have one more thing, and we'll be using it tonight." More? "This." This was the oldest looking and probably thickest book I'd ever seen. She plopped it right on the glass table. "This is our coven's Book of Magic. Now this has been around for hundreds of years—each new generation adding more to it. I've already looked up what we'll need for tonight, but after that, it's yours."

"Ours?" Maia and I said together.

"Well yes, you're the next generation. You will have much to learn from this book—and hopefully much to add... Girls I'm still dead, it's not my book to use anymore."

I was staring in awe, from the wands, to Maia, back to the book and Bridget. "Bridget. This is all incredible… But do you think we're ready?"

"I know we haven't had a chance to do a lot of actual training, but you both are about to help bring down The Reaper and destroy The Crypt. I'd say that well earns these." She paused a moment, allowing us to take it all in. "But now, we have plans to discuss. Are you girls ready to do this?" She leaned forward in her seat, ready to get into it.

The most important night of our lives. The wands, the book, the night dresses, the planning, Bridget had talked about ceremonies—this felt like a coming of age, a rite of passage challenge honestly.

We'd spent the past several hours going over every detail—where, how, when, specific timing, and most importantly, what happened if anything went wrong. AKA: Maddie. Bridget and Maia both agreed to my decision, we could no longer trust her on any level, whether she showed up or not.

Now, as the clock struck midnight, we were getting ready and there was still no word from Maddie. I didn't care. There was nothing she could say at this point anyway.

"Is this better? More suitable for a proper ritual?" Maia asked Bridget as we both gave a twirl. Maia had found a black sundress to pair with Mary Jane flats. Not her normal style, but she would deal with it for tonight. I had found a simple knee length gothic style dress. The bottom had a layered flow that turned into a tighter lace fit coming up to my neck. We'd also ventured off earlier for maybe an hour to see if we could find any suitable accessories. We couldn't help it. We'd had the time and I didn't want to miss the chance to at least see a bit of the town while we were here.

The townspeople were very friendly. Every shop owner greeted us as we entered and seemed to quickly notice that we weren't from around here. Maybe it was the clothes, the accent, or our demeanor, I couldn't quite tell. But they seemed very interested in life outside Salem.

Though one thing did strike me as odd. Each shop, once they learned our names, gave us the same expression the worker at the witchery back home had given me the first day I'd gone in. This dumbfounded look of shock that I didn't quite understand.

We didn't last long in any shop after that look. But we did find two pairs of lacy black gloves—only coming to our wrists. Perfectly fitting with the dresses.

"They're perfect... Oh it's like a true ceremony for the dead—awakening of lost souls." Bridget had her arms crossed but was still smiling at us. "Only one thing. Lose the gloves."

"Huh? Oh." Maia slightly pouted, looking down at her hands. "I thought they were such a nice touch though."

"They're beautiful gloves. Wonderful for any other day in Salem. But you need the full capacity of your abilities and to stay in control over them. Gloves hinder you."

"Oh, sure. I guess I hadn't thought about that." Maia began pulling off the gloves. "I'll find some other use maybe."

"We'll find a way to put them to good use." Bridget gave Maia a wink.

"Ok, gloves off. But we do need to go, if we want to have things started by the witching hour. We're still making good time right now."

Everything in this town was so close together, it didn't take any longer than ten minutes to drive to Proctor's Ledge Memorial. The original site of demise.

Seeing it now, refreshed and restructured, it was hard to believe such horrible practices and punishments had taken place hundreds of years ago.

"It looks so peaceful now, so strange." Bridget. We knew what had happened to her but I still often forgot.

This place wasn't new to her, just renewed. The spot where her own village had turned on her. She was a healer—helping so many with ailments and that's how she was repaid. Not thanked. Hung. Viewed as wicked. How could the same people who had been suffering, the ones she healed, look at her as a such a monster?

"They thought if I was the one making them better, I had to be the one making them sick. It was all about money—that's how it was painted."

Centuries. For centuries! It never fails. It's always about power or money.

We'd pulled off to the side of the road and just sat for a moment. Letting Bridget take her time. I don't know how I'd react in the same situation—confronting the very place I'd been murdered. She had yet to cease to amaze me.

"Thank you for allowing me the moment. We can go now."

"Wait just a second." Maia had pulled out her phone. "I think there might be a better place." Bridget and I both waited for her to continue. "This just feels a little too out in the open... There's a park just across the street and it looks like they have a hiking trail. We could go there?"

Bridget had a look on her face, considering it. "I guess we don't have to do it at the exact location—as long as we're close enough."

"Across the street feels pretty close to me, but can we get in? It might be closed at night."

"We might not have to worry about that... I mean, I can get in no problem, but Aly. You can make things move. Do you want to see if you can move more than just a candle or a curtain?"

I looked from her to Maia. "You think I can teleport into the park?"

"I think you can try and take Maia with you. It's already getting close to two o'clock, so we don't have much time either. Why not give it a try?" We'd spent the last couple hours getting dressed and prepared before coming out. We needed to be here for the witching hour, but there was no point in being hours early.

I sucked in a breath, "Uhh, ok. You need to bring the other stuff then." Bridget actually gave a thumbs up... A thumbs up. Ok.

I closed my eyes and opened my hand for Maia to take. I needed to channel my energy and focus in on what I wanted. I wanted the park, the trails, the forest, I started painting the picture—what it might feel like, smell like. It was all similar to The Crypt, only now there was more dim light from the moon and not such a heavy darkness looming around you.

As the image became clearer I felt a warm tingle trickling down my neck, meeting the base and flowing to my shoulders. The more I painted, the more trees I added, the longer I made the dirt path, the stronger and warmer the tingle got. Driving its way down my arms and into my fingers, until finally connecting with Maia.

"Oh, whoa." She was feeling it now too.

"Yes, keep going." Bridget encouraged.

I just had to push us through, into that painted image. One rush of energy, that's all it took.

Opening my eyes, there we were. On the other edge of the woods. I did it. We were on the park trails and I was left blinking in shock.

"Well done, Aly. This connection ritual should be a piece of cake." Bridget had joined us, standing to the side, giving room for our arrival.

"Wow. I really just did that."

Then with a smile and a curtsy, Bridget handed me my wand. *I think I was just knighted.*

Still no word from Maddie. No one cared. Even if she did show up now, we were in a closed park—she couldn't get in.

"Do you think we'll see her?" Maia asked.

"If she's back in The Crypt." Bridget was matter of fact. "But we've gone over the plan, we're here to finish this."

We had the Book of Magic set up, with Bridget's specifically sorted notes, and Maia and I were set with our wands. We may not have Maddie's energy but now, with these wands, screw her.

"Now, you'll both need access to the wands, but stay together. So Aly, take Maia's hand and no matter what, don't let go. You need to draw your energy together."

We nodded and obliged.

It was almost time to begin.

Bridget took one slow breath, "This is a big moment girls. We are about to take down what has been known as the death prison for witches for centuries. We are saving witches that did nothing but try to help people through their short lives. Save poor lost souls who are trying to find their way back home again. We are about to make sure no person or witch has to suffer or endure the torture of The Crypt again."

I squeezed Maia's hand for not just comfort but excitement and reassurance.

"Now, before I go in and start gathering the souls, there's one last thing to say... No matter what happens today, I'm honored that I was chosen as your future mentor. I am so happy I got to meet you both and am able to help you in this life-changing journey. However that being said, if anything does start going south and the only way to stop things is to close the portal or destroy it early and I'm still there—do not hesitate." She looked directly at me then. "I'm serious. Do not hesitate."

Tears stung my eyes at the thought, but I couldn't let them show. Bridget was right. She looked at me because she knew I would've said the same thing.

"We won't. And, Bridget, thank you for everything you've done for us." That's all I could muster for now. We all needed to make it out of this. Then I could tell her the rest.

She gave me a solemn nod, and then she was gone.

Chapter 21

Maia and I were left in silence. My whole body tensed, waiting on Bridget's cue. It was already pitch black outside, the only light coming from the full moon. The night air was cold and still besides the sporadic light breezes that sent chills down my spine when they made it past the trees.

On Bridget's cue, I needed to open the portal, bridging our world to The Crypt. With Maia's tracking ability we'd found a way to amplify that through the Book of Magic. Thankfully, there had been many trackers to make discoveries in the past. Because once the portal was open, Maia needed to charm it for any soul traveling through that still had a living body.

Any soul who still had a body healing, if everything went as planned, wouldn't be stepping through to meet us. They'd be going home. Another reason Bridget needed to gather everyone. She needed to tell them what to do when they got out.

We had walked Maddie through the process, but this was just too many. If we wanted to do this in time, we just needed to get them out. But, if this worked, we could save them all…

The coven witches, however, wouldn't have any bodies to go back to. The charm wouldn't affect them. They would all join us here.

It was such a simple and perfect plan. An easy plan. If we didn't have any interruptions.

"How long do you think it'll take?" Maia said, breaking what had felt like an eternity of silence.

I took a slow, deep breath, "I don't know—we saw the souls in the field that day, but I don't know if that was all of them. She could be gathering twenty people or more than a hundred."

"Plus the coven." Maia pointed out.

"Yes, plus the coven."

"You weren't going to start without me, were you?" Maddie's voice suddenly rang out from behind us.

"Maddie?" We both flipped a 180 to see her suddenly appear at the trailhead, walking toward us. "We didn't think you were coming." I shot Maia a look that I hoped

Maddie didn't notice—even from her short distance left to cross.

"I tried reaching out but I couldn't seem to get through. Neither one of you could hear me." She looked down as she joined us, not far from the entrance. "You have wands now! A gift from Bridget?"

She wasn't doing a great job of hiding her strange demeanor.

"Yea, they were our ancestors—kept safe since the trials." Maia asserted.

"Oh! Do you think she'd have mine?"

I shook my head, confused. "Sorry, Maddie, how did you know where to find us?"

"Yea, also, you said you tried to reach out. We didn't hear you at all. We didn't even sense someone *attempting* to connect. What happened?"

"It was strange. Yes, I tried reaching out to let you know I'd worked it out and was on my way. I tried again when I got here but both times I got nothing. I've never done the bond thing before so I don't really know how to explain it... It was like mentally knocking on a brick wall."

What an interesting thing to say...

"But you still came?" I made myself feign shock.

"Well of course! If you were coming to Salem, I figured, something this important, you'd be going back to the original site. But, when you weren't there, the only other option was close by and secluded."

"Huh. That's dedication." I scoffed, but honestly, I was impressed. She was convincing. "Damn."

"Like I've been telling you—I'm here to help. We need to make sure that cell stays closed and I know you can use my energy."

"About that!" Maia, now excited for the chance to show off her wand. "Because we weren't sure if you'd come, these were early gifts."

"So you helping with that cell may be the biggest help of all actually." I shifted from Maia's excitement back to Maddie. "We're waiting on Bridget's cue. Once the portal's open, you could go right in and make sure that sticks."

"Oh." Maddie paused, shifting her feet. "You want me to go in and just stand guard?"

"How else do you make sure it stays closed?" What was she planning to do? Tackle her if she got free and tried to leave? "Bridget is in there now, so you'd both get out together before we close it. If we stick to the plan you have nothing to worry about. *We* always stand by our word." I couldn't help but take the slight dig. It also wasn't a lie—that *was* the original plan. Not our fault she went off script.

"Uhm. Ok. Sure. If that was the plan." She was hesitant but I could tell she was forcing herself to go along.

What was in this for her, really? Was it really as simple as being promised a mentor for her powers? That just seemed so small. Not to downplay Bridget, but we weren't trying to take over an underworld so she'd train us.

"Will you be able to handle that?" Maia said with the slightest overdose of snark—enough for me to squeeze her hand. "We want to make sure you're comfortable too."

I felt Maia's mental eyeroll down the bond, "Better?"

"We just need to get her in there and distracted."

"Yes, yes, I can do it. No problem."

"Great. Now everyone, shut up and wait for Bridget's cue." I needed to regain control of this. Bridget would be calling any minute. "We have one shot. Maddie, stand here behind us and I'll tell you when."

She gave a silent nod and Maia took my hand back as we all, once again, fell silent. Waiting.

Closing my eyes, I squeezed Maia's hand and whispered down the bond. "Start pooling, Maia. We need to build our energy together." My hand started feeling her warmth, all the acknowledgement I needed. She was pushing her energy towards me, connecting to me. Accepting hers and pushing my own back sent the wildest tingles up my arm, through my shoulder, and down my spine—until I was feeling something of a surge through my whole body. This was exactly what we needed. With each other and our wands, we became unstoppable.

I could hear the wind, the trees rustling behind us, crickets chirping, and other little bugs from the trail. But nothing was distracting. Nothing could take my attention away. Then I heard it.

"Aly, we're ready." Bridget's cue.

"It's time, Maia." I opened my eyes but I only focused on where I needed to place the portal. "I'm opening the portal and then it's your go." She only gave me another hand squeeze. That's all I needed.

One shot. That's all we had. Get everyone out, then Bridget, and seal the portal. We brought everything we could to prevent us from being tracked but who knew if it was enough. Once that portal was open—once souls were leaving, he would know.

My hand was shaking as I raised my wand, but I had my image set, just like in that hospital room. I could already imagine all the freed spirits bursting through that portal window to find themselves again—back to their human forms. I didn't know who they were, or what their names were, but the image alone gave me such joy. The joy of reuniting with not just someone they thought was gone forever, but a whole life they almost lost. This was a feeling I didn't want to let go of.

Just like at the hospital, as I focused on the images and the emotions intensified, that window only grew bigger and bigger. Finally, that blinding light shot free from the wand—opening into the same glowing portal as I'd opened before.

"Yes! It worked!" I screamed when Bridget came clear into view. "Crescere! Crescere!" I directed the words with the wand towards the portal once more.

These were just a few words I'd learned from the Book of Magic to make sure the portal would grow once I'd created it.

"Maddie, go! Before Maia charms it." She hesitated only a moment, then sprinted. I had to smirk—he was going to be pissed.

Maddie leapt through—a bit dramatic but whatever got her in there—and kept sprinting past Bridget.

"She actually showed up? And you convinced her?" Bridget sent quickly down the bond. She was impressed. "Well done."

"What can I say? I can be pretty persuasive when I want to be." I gave a little shrug at her.

"I don't even want to know. Let's just get on with it."

"Ok, Maia, you're up!"

"Yes. Right." Raising her wand. She looked much more confident than I had. "Suscipe me in domum suam!" Again. "Suscipe me in domum suam!" Nothing shot out from hers though... Instead a soft purple glow sat lighting it up as if giving it an aura.

"What's happening?"

"Tap the portal!" Bridget sent down the bond. I didn't know how loud anything was on her side—this portal sounded like the buzz of a fluorescent lamp over here.

"Just stand on the side of it and tap on the edge." Maia obeyed.

Stepping to the side, as soon as her wand connected with the edge everything turned a warm lavender purple. It made sense, like a welcome home color.

Maia started pumping her wand hand in the air. She'd be clapping but our hands couldn't disconnect.

"Ok everyone, go!" Bridget ordered the spirits who started hustling forward.

One after the other, running towards the portal, disappearing on contact. Each time sending a wave of lavender rippling back through the portal wall. It was really working... We were really saving them!

Three spirits, now four, five! All stepping through and vanishing. All going back to their human bodies. Six, seven, eight—I was losing track the faster they came.

"Halfway through!" Bridget called.

The excitement was burning in me—my eyes already stinging with tears. We still had the witches, hold it together! We were so close!

"Wait, did you hear that?" Bridget paused just as the last soul was crossing the finish line.

"Hear what?" I asked, everything had been fine—no creeping tension, no feelings, no one busting out in an ambush.

But then I did hear it. The caw.

"Bridget. Hurry!" Now I was screaming through the portal. "We have to keep moving." We only had the witches left now! We were so close dammit!

Everything had come to a screeching halt at the sound of that damned crow.

Another caw—this time loud enough to vibrate the entire portal and echo inside my head. Shit. He had to be getting closer. Bridget was at a loss trying to help the others, whose feet had seemingly become glued to the forest floor. No one was getting out.

"Now, you didn't think I could really let this happen now did you?" There it was—from caw to the voice, the dark, cloaked and shadowed figure came into view behind Bridget. "Silly, silly girl. Ambitious, but so naive."

Suddenly, the witches waiting to get through that portal weren't just frozen, they were shackled.

"What do you want from me?" I wanted to sound more confident but I couldn't hide my pent up rage.

"You really haven't figured that out by now?"

I raised my brow and threw my hands up. "Can we stop talking in these bullshit riddles? Obviously not."

"Suit yourself if you want to sell yourself short. I've been trying to get you here."

"That answers nothing. What do you want with me?"

"It's not about what I want with you, Aly. It's about where you're meant to be."

Where I was meant to be? How could I be meant to be in The Crypt? That made no sense.

"Don't listen to him, Aly. He doesn't know what he's talking about." She turned to address The Reaper directly, "She does *not* belong in this hellhole."

"Bridget? What is he talking about?"

"Oh, did she not tell you?" Now he was taunting me. "Here let me just show you a peek."

Before I could object, he was in my mind and images were flashing. The Crypt. Souls. Then darkness and I was moving. Through The Crypt, through what seemed like a passage, into darkness. Moving so slowly, like I was mentally tiptoeing, up toward the back of what looked like a throne—a cloak draped over the side.

Another flash, suddenly I was facing the throne, staring at the dark, cloaked figure. Still hidden by the darkness, their hood raised up and over just the same as The Reaper. I could see nothing but long, feminine fingers tapping on the armrests. Then suddenly a cruel smile appeared under the hood.

I was in a memory... The Reaper's memory. But could this other figure actually see me?

Another flash—now I was in the corner, across from the throne, placed out of the way to watch.

Was this really where his leader stayed? There had to be more than this. What were they hiding if *this* is what they wanted me to see?

My mind was spiraling. Then, The Reaper I knew suddenly appeared, and he wasn't alone.

With him, he had two souls, walking towards the throne. My breath caught—he was showing me what happened to those poor souls in The Crypt... When their time ended... He was delivering them.

The throned figure sat in silence, examining the offering before them. Seeming pleased, they stood up and lowered their hood.

My eyes widened staring at that familiar face. My breath caught in my throat. *This* is what he wanted to show me?

"It's me?"

The Reaper, turning in my direction, lowered his hood and smiled.

"Maia?"

Then I watched myself breathe the remaining life out of the poor soul standing before them. The Reaper's offering.

I couldn't breathe. I couldn't move. I couldn't understand. "Please, make it stop."

"This is your destiny, Aly. This is who you are." The images and memories stopped and I was back on the trail looking at The Reaper through the portal.

"No. It's not!" I screamed.

That was never going to happen. I wouldn't let it. "*That* is not me. *You* are not Maia."

"What?" Maia hadn't seen anything I'd just been shown.

"Aly, I made a deal with Maddie. But I'll make a better one with you." I was seething, but I was also stuck. Apparently, right about Maddie, the coven was stuck, and this was actually our fault in another sense of the word?

"What's your deal?" I demanded.

"Maddie is going to release that witch and we both know you don't want that. My offer? I'll free these witches and lock Maddie in with the mentor she wants so badly. All you have to do? Join me in here."

I was frozen, "Join you and become that creature you showed me?"

"And live up to your fullest potential."

"Don't do it, Aly. Remember, *do not hesitate.*"

"Bridget, did you know about this?"

"I'm growing impatient and that little brat should be releasing your witch any minute now." The Reaper looked at their wrist as if looking at a watch.

"Do not hesitate, Aly!" Bridget screamed now.

But I did hesitate. Maddie could be locked up, the coven would be released and so would Bridget. It would only be my own sacrifice. I hesitated. But someone else didn't.

I hadn't even noticed a witch off to the side who hadn't been shackled. The witch who stepped forward just as

Maddie was bursting from the trees in the far end of the field. It happened so fast I could hardly react.

"You're meant for more than this, girls. I know you'll figure this out. I love you!" Spoken so quickly, from a mouth I never expected, but could never forget. Then I watched my mother close the portal herself.

"Mom?" I could barely whisper the word.

"Aly, we have to seal it."

I lifted my wand again, towards the slightest glimmer left from the portal. "Sub Caelo lunari et decreto sagarum, vos obsigno, ne quis exeat." And with that, the glimmer was gone.

We both stood there in silence, speechless for some time. We'd done everything right, taken every precaution, made every backup plan, but still it all had gone so wrong.

Finally, I looked at Maia, taking her face in my hands. "Maia. This isn't over. The Crypt is only sealed, not destroyed. The Reaper is still out there and Bridget is gone. But we are going to get her back, we're going to find mom again, and most importantly, we will not become them."

About the Author

Originally from the PNW, Molly found herself starting her own businesses before eventually returning to the arts and falling back in love with writing. With a passion for exploration, travel, and the mysteries of the paranormal, she now channels those curiosities into her stories. This is just the beginning of her journey into the world of storytelling—and she's only just getting started.

Stay tuned for book 2

Revenge of The Reaper